Family Matters

Fortune Bay novella

Judith Hudson

SPOILER ALERT!

Be sure to read **The Good Neighbor** before

reading this novella!

Hi Everyone!

When I finished writing *Home for Christmas*, Louise and Blue's story, I sat back and thought about where everyone in Fortune Bay was in their lives at this point. Louise and Blue were fine, all lovey-dovely, Louise moving into Blue's new log house, both of them ecstatic about the possibility of twins.

But what about Frankie and Sean? By spring, it had been five months since they found Amber—or rather, since she found Sean. Now he and Amber were living with his mom Stephanie, and Frankie was living alone— not the best situation for Sean and Frankie – or for Stephanie and Max.

And what about Amber? It was hard to believe everything was just smooth sailing for her after such a huge upheaval in her life.

By now you have probably figured out how real these characters are to me! Lol. I couldn't leave them in this situation. The story started to grow and turned into this sequel novella, written specially for my most loyal readers who have been reading all the Murphy family Fortune Bay books.

If you haven't read the other books, do yourself a favor and put this book aside until you have.

I hope you enjoy *Family Matters as much as I enjoyed writing it!*

Judy Hudson

The Fortune Bay Series

Lake of Dreams
Get this free prequel e-novella when you sign up for my readers group at
bit.ly/freeFB-e-book

Summer of Fortune
Book One

The Good Neighbor
Book Two

Home for Christmas
Book Three

Family Matters
A Sequel Novella

Starting Over
Book Four

Starlight and Tinsel
A Christmas Novella

Also by Judith Hudson

The Secret at Elk Horn Lodge

Chapter 1

Sean geared down his Miata and cranked the wheel, turning into his mother's driveway. Slamming the gearshift into park, he sat, hands gripping the steering wheel and listened to the rain drumming on the convertible roof as he tried to pull himself together. No sense tackling his daughter Amber in his current mood of... what? Anger? Frustration? He blew out a breath, trying to force the hot ball of anxiety out of his chest. He couldn't lose her again.

But what was wrong with the girl? He'd lost his baby girl when he was sixteen and it had been eating at him ever since. Now he'd finally found her and had full custody, but from there his plan had gone off the rails. It wasn't the fairy tale scenario he'd dreamed of; she wasn't the sweet little girl he'd imagined. The real Amber was tough, a scared, damaged fifteen-year-old who for some reason seemed to be fighting him every inch of the way, when all he wanted was to make her life easy. Give her everything she'd been denied before, starting with a safe, secure, loving home. If only she'd let him.

He opened the car door and made a dash for the house, kicking his wet shoes off inside the door.

"That you, Sean?" His mother's voice echoed

down the hall.

Living in each other's pockets was wearing thin, but he couldn't have managed without her these past five months.

Stephanie Murphy sat at the cluttered kitchen table, a mish mash of her art supplies scattered before her, having a quiet before-dinner drink with her good friend, Sean's boss, Max.

He felt bad about disrupting their quiet interlude, but there was no alternative. "Where's Amber?"

Stephanie's eyebrows went up. "She's not home yet."

Sean clenched his jaw and ground his teeth. This was becoming a bad habit he hoped he wasn't going to pay for in future dental bills. He blew out a breath and forced himself to relax. "The school phoned. She's been skipping classes."

Stephanie's shoulders fell. "Not again."

Sean ran a hand through his short, cropped hair. "Where the hell is she?"

Stephanie glanced at the clock. "I assumed she went over to Brandy's."

"We can't assume anything with her these days. I bet she's out with that boy."

The back door opened, and Amber stepped into the kitchen, stopping in the spotlight scrutiny of the three adults. "What?"

"Where have you been?" Sean snapped. Stephanie winced.

"At Brandy's. You said I could go there after school if I was home for dinner."

"How did you get there?"

Her eyes flashed away then back. "School bus."

Sean's eyes narrowed. He didn't think so, but short of calling Brandy's mom, he couldn't prove otherwise. And checking up on her like that, like he thought she was lying, was no way to build bridges.

He chose a different tack. "The school called. They said you weren't at your afternoon classes."

Amber's face hardened. "I went to class all morning, but that's all I could stand. It's just too hard. My brain gets tired. I have to get out."

"What's too hard, dear?" Stephanie asked.

"I can't concentrate for hours on end. Sometimes I just have to get away."

Sean stepped toward her. "Well you can go up to your room now and do the work you missed in class today. And come directly home after school every day this week."

"Fine!" Amber stormed out of the room. Sean stared down the empty hall, his back rigid, until her bedroom door slammed upstairs. Then he slumped into a chair and rubbed his face with the palm of his hand.

Stephanie held up her glass in a toast. "Welcome to the wonderful world of teenage children."

Sean shook his head. "I blew it. But what does she mean, *it's too hard*? If she'd go to class, it might not be so hard."

"There's bound to be a transition time when

you change schools." Stephanie said. "And she's changed more than schools. Her whole life has changed. Give her a bit more time."

"You're right." Sean looked at her out of the corner of his eye. "Mind if I go out for a while? We probably shouldn't leave Amber alone."

"Sorry," Stephanie said, downing her drink and rising a bit too eagerly from her chair. "Max and I have plans. We won't be late."

Sean sighed. "I know. She's my responsibility. I am doing my best."

Stephanie put her hand on his shoulder as she walked by him. "I know you are. Don't be too hard on yourself. You two are still getting to know each other. You have no history to go by, no way of knowing what she'll do next. Or why. Give yourself some time, too."

"You're right," he said, but without conviction as the older couple got their coats and went out into the rain, leaving Sean in the quiet kitchen.

His mother's kitchen. He'd moved back in when Amber showed up on their doorstep last fall, thrilled to have found her and grateful to his mother for offering them a haven. Neutral ground where he'd hoped they could slowly get to know each other.

But five months in and he was no closer to understanding this girl. *His girl.* Her outright rejection of the love he was trying to give her was tearing him apart.

He pulled out his phone and called Frankie. He wasn't seeing nearly enough of her these days, but between his responsibilities with Amber, and the new job…

"Hi." Frankie's bright tone turned the hurt in his heart into longing. A longing that wasn't going to be sated tonight.

"Hi."

She waited a beat and when she spoke, the fun had gone out of her voice. "Oh, no. Not again. What now?"

"The school called. She's been skipping again."

"Not my class." Frankie taught English at the local high school and Amber was enrolled in her tenth grade English class this semester.

"She probably knows I'd find out about that right away."

"How did you deal with it?"

"Grounded her for a week."

"Hmmm. Want me to come over?"

"Yes. No. Mom went out and Amber's sulking in her room. I should probably go up and talk to her. Not that I know what to say or think it will do any good. We haven't had dinner yet, either."

"Okay," Frankie said, the disappointment in her voice pointing to one more failure in his life. He felt he was failing Frankie, Amber, his mother, everyone.

"Hey, I'm really sorry. This is not what I want for us, either."

"I know. Maybe tomorrow?"

"I'll try. I love you."

"Yeah, me too," she said, but the warmth in her voice he remembered was missing, and then she hung up the phone.

He hated to put Frankie on the back burner, but what could he do? Before Amber had shown up on his doorstep last fall, he'd had plans—a house, marriage, a family with Frankie. He'd tried to bring Frankie and Amber together, but Amber had resisted all of Frankie's overtures of friendship. Sometimes he wondered if she was jealous of their relationship?

He was tired of juggling these balls in the air, and wasn't doing a good job of it, either. Every other day one of them burst into flame and he either burnt his hands or dropped it completely. Then he was back at square one.

He'd gotten what he wanted, his daughter back, but hoped it wasn't at the cost of the woman he loved.

Chapter 2

Frankie stood in her dining room with her phone in her hand, looking out the window at pelting rain and angry waves crashing onto the shore of Fortune Bay. It was time to call in the troops. She punched her friends Maddie and Louise's numbers into the phone and sent out the text. *Can you get away tonight?*

An hour later, her friends had arrived, and Frankie was sitting with them at her dining room table, eating the tiny sandwiches and cookies Louise had brought and drinking sparkling pink lemonade in solidarity with her two pregnant friends.

Louise had just taken a sip of her drink, when Frankie blurted, "I think Sean and I are breaking up." The words tumbled out their own accord.

Louise nearly choked on her drink. The thought had been growing in Frankie's mind for weeks now, and a melancholy blanket of relief settled over her hearing it said aloud. If anyone would give her honest feedback it would be Louise and Maddie.

"No," both women exclaimed in unison.

"Sean's been busy," Maddie said, her brow furrowed in concern.

Frankie nodded, managing to shake her head at

the same time, the gesture echoing her internal confusion. "I've said the same thing myself. But still…"

Louise set her glass down on the coffee table and leaned forward. "He's had a lot on his plate ever since you two got together. First the job at the resort, and almost simultaneously finding Amber. The adjustment has been tough on them both. Having a baby is crazy enough," she said, patting her baby bump. "I can't imagine having a fifteen-year-old daughter suddenly appear in your life. At least I have nine months to prepare."

"You're right. I know. I get why he moved back in with Stephanie when Amber arrived. We weren't living together. Not officially. He had some of his things here and some next door at the cabin. It would have been too awkward for him to live there alone with a fifteen-year-old daughter he'd never met. And I respect him immensely for taking her in and for taking on the challenge of being a father. But does it have to mean we never have any time together anymore?"

"And then, the job," Maddie said. "Publicity Director—it's a big opportunity."

"And it's perfect for him," Louise added.

"I know, I know," Frankie said, hating the whine in her voice. "But work is sucking up every available minute he's not with Amber. That would be okay if we were living together and could talk in the evening and crawl into bed together every night. These days, though, that hardly ever happens. It's not like we have a long history. We had really just gotten together—and now he's drifting away."

"I don't think he's drifting," Maddie said, looking tentatively at Louise for support. "I think he's treading water, barely keeping his head above the surface. Amber needs a lot of support and," she paused, bit her lip, searching for the right word, "*guidance* right now."

Frankie nodded. "I've been telling myself the same thing for the past five months, that the situation is temporary, that he still loves me and is there for me, just not *here* very often. Less often all the time. I know Amber has a lot to get used to, they both do, but I could help him, help them both, if he'd only let me. I had just gotten used to him being here and then he was whisked away into this whole new life which, unfortunately, doesn't seem have a place for me."

"Amber's a good kid," Louise said emphatically. "It has to be hard settling into a new home. She just needs time to adjust. I know she seems tough on the outside, but she and Brandy helped me a lot with the baking for the Christmas sale. Brandy might be my sister but she's not much of a baker. Amber, on the other hand, is a natural. She's really interested in helping me set up the pastry department at the resort this summer."

"I know. Sean appreciates the time you've spent with Amber," Frankie said. "And I guess that's part of the problem. You and Amber get along so well, but she and I have never... bonded."

It was hard to admit. After all, she was an English teacher at Majestic High and worked with teenagers every day. As the learning professional of the group, she felt she should be able to deal with Amber. Instead, she felt like everything she did only made things worse.

"Maybe if you invited her over," Maddie suggested, easing her own baby bump out from between the chair and the table.

Frankie shook her head. "Sean brought her over a few times at first, but she was so obviously uncomfortable that he started leaving her at Stephanie's and coming by himself. Since Christmas, though, he's come less and less." She threw up her hands. "I get it, he's crazy busy at the resort." She rested an elbow on the table and her chin in her hand. "But I miss him."

"Easter weekend is only a month away," Maddie said. "Once the resort opens, I'm sure he'll have more free time."

"I guess. But the problem with Amber has gotten even worse since she started taking my English class this semester. She's just not doing the work, hasn't completed one full assignment. I don't even know if she's even reading the books. And the work she hands in is way below tenth grade level. She can hardly look me in the eye."

"I've spent a lot of time with her," Louise added. "She's a smart kid."

"But have you seen her spelling?" Frankie asked.

"You can be smart and not know how to spell,"

Louise said staunchly.

"I know, but terrible spelling is an indicator of something. I have been trying to cut her some slack, I know how hard this transition must be, but I'm her teacher and at some point I have to assign her a mark. The way it looks now, she won't be passing."

Louise's brows went up. "Sean will love that."

"I don't know how to tell him," Frankie said morosely. "I'm trying to leave school at school and home at home, but it's almost impossible. I'll talk to Amber on Monday."

"Give it some time," Maddie said, helping herself to a cucumber sandwich. "She'll come around."

Frankie nodded, but felt that Maddie didn't quite get it. She had always been so maternal, such a natural mother, she didn't understand how awkward Frankie felt around Amber.

Frankie had always seen herself as an independent career woman, had a good job, owned her own house, and thought she had enough of kids at school. She had been completely content—until last fall. Then Sean Murphy came into her life and Maddie *and* Louise both announced they were pregnant. Now, at seven months Maddie was glowing. Louise was six months along and having twins, so her belly was quickly catching up to Maddie's in girth. They were both so darn happy... When those two were together, the air was thick with a rich brew of maternal pheromones, and Frankie could feel it beginning to rub off on her.

Baby envy. Not just baby envy but family envy. She wanted it all, the whole shebang: husband, family, a baby of her own. Suddenly, the traditional family unit looked pretty darn appealing. But she couldn't confide her longing to her friends. Not now. Not when her future with Sean was on such shaky ground.

She was willing to accept Amber into their family unit, but a fifteen-year-old stepdaughter, with issues, was not at all the same thing as a baby. And since Amber arrived, Frankie's dreams of home and family seemed to have been pushed out of the way. She felt like she was alone, out there in the deep end treading water, but not in the same pool as Sean.

By nine o'clock Maddie and Louise were yawning and toddled off home. Frankie appreciated her friends trying to reassure her, but she knew things between her and Sean just weren't right. Covering the plate of sandwiches, she put them in the refrigerator and wiped the crumbs off the granite countertop that divided the kitchen from the living room. When she turned out the kitchen light, the lamplight from the living room gave the brushed stainless appliances a warm glow.

Her kitchen wasn't getting much use these days. Frankie had never cooked but thought fondly back to the days last summer when Sean moved into the cabin next door and they were first getting to know each other. He came over occasionally with fresh-caught fish and using the veggies from Frankie's garden, had cooked delicious dinners for them both.

Then, in the autumn, things had progressed between them and he'd cooked and eaten dinner with her almost every night. He'd parked his boat at her dock, moved his electric piano into her living room and brought over his TV until finally, their friends started asking if he had moved in.

She'd gotten used to having him there, had *loved* having him there, had thought they'd had a future together. Then he found Amber and everything changed. They moved into Stephanie's house, he got the job at the resort—and she hardly saw him anymore.

She was happy for him, she really was, but she missed him. In a few short months last fall they'd started to build a life together. Now she was afraid the dream was falling to pieces—and she didn't know how to stop it.

Chapter 3

Frankie locked the doors, picked up her book and was heading for bed when a knock sounded on the sliding patio door and Sean's tired face smiled through the glass. She slid open the door for him and although the air outside was cool, she felt a rush of warmth as he stepped inside. "I didn't think I'd see you tonight."

Sean's short blonde hair and crystal-blue eyes were the same as always, but the exhausted droop of his shoulders was new. He kissed her lightly on the cheek. "Mom came home so I thought I'd take a chance and drop by."

Putting an arm around her waist, he led her back to the kitchen. Frankie perched on a stool at the marble counter and watched as he opened the fridge door.

"Anything left to eat?" Pulling out the foil-covered plate with the last few sandwiches and cookies, he mumbled, "Thank you, Louise," as he stuffed a tiny party sandwich into his mouth.

Frankie smiled. "Maddie and Louise were here, but they didn't last too long. They just give each other permission to flake out early. I don't mind, though. You look tired, too."

"I am. I didn't really eat any dinner. Too stressed." He pulled two stemmed glasses out of the cupboard and opened a bottle of wine. "Let's sit down." Taking the plate and the glasses, they headed into the living room.

"Do you really need to stay home with Amber all the time?" Frankie asked. "She is fifteen. She could be alone for a while in the evening."

Sean took Frankie's hand and pulled her down beside him onto the couch. "Old enough to get into trouble. I came home one night last week and she wasn't there. No note, and she wasn't next door at Brandy's. I was beginning to worry when she came through the door, said she had been out with 'the girls' but I know she was with that guy she's been hanging around."

"You've got to expect that. She's so pretty—all that long blonde hair—the guys are bound to be interested."

"But she's only fifteen. This guy's way too old. He's big, got to be a senior. And driving. I worry about her."

Frankie knew the boy Sean was talking about. He had been in her class the year before. He was at least two years older than Amber, and he did look tough, had a couple of tattoos and shaggy black hair, but it was his attitude, the way the other kids cleared the way when he walked down the hall, that set him apart. "Probably wise to worry. If you can do it without her thinking you're spying on her."

Sean nodded. "That would only get her back up. We've had enough run-ins that turned into shouting matches. I'm never sure who wins.

Mom's a big help, though."

Frankie bit her lip. "I wish I could help."

Sean winced. "I know. Amber's not very comfortable around you yet. Once the resort is open, we'll plan some fun outings. Just the three of us."

He pulled her in for a hug and she melted against him. When they were together like this, it seemed like everything might work out. Their lips met with a heat that drove everything else from her mind. She wove her fingers through his thick curly hair, and he pulled her closer, deepening the kiss. Holding her neck with one hand, his other hand worked its way under her loose linen blouse. His hand was warm and sure, and she arched her back as he tickled his way up her spine, found the clasp on her bra and—

A knock on the door jarred them out of their trance. Frankie glanced across the kitchen to the clock and saw it was after ten. Late for guests. "Now what?"

Disentangling herself from his arms with regret, allowing him one last kiss, she walked over and opened the front door, totally unprepared for the sight of her father, Philip Alvarez, standing on her doorstep.

"Hi, honey." Stepping inside, he pulled his startled daughter into a one-armed hug, planting a kiss on her forehead.

"Dad, what are you doing here?"

Phillip set down his duffle bag and spread his arms. "I've sold the business. I'm moving to

Fortune Bay."

Frankie's mind raced and her mouth fell open. "But…"

Philip closed the door, picked up his bag and walked into the living room, Frankie trailing behind him in a daze.

"Hi Sean. Sorry to interrupt."

Sean had stood up and held out a hand to shake. "Good to see you, Philip. Did I hear you say you're moving here?"

Frankie finally found her voice. "I thought you weren't going to retire for a couple of years."

"A good offer came up and I thought, why wait. You've landed on a gold mine here, honey. This town is ripe for development."

"How did you get here? I didn't hear the float plane." The last few times her dad had visited— actually, the only two times, both since their reconciliation last fall—he'd flown from Seattle airport in a rented float plane.

"I drove. From Chicago. Bought a brand-new Mercedes 4X4. It's a beauty. Packed up some stuff and headed out. I wanted to surprise you."

Frankie laughed. "Consider me surprised. Amazed, actually."

He looked at the two wine glasses on the coffee table, tilted his head and winced. "I'm interrupting. I could probably get a room at the resort, even though I know it's not open yet, but I was hoping I could stay here—just for a while— until I find a place and get settled."

Get settled. That raised any number of questions. *What are you going to do? Where are you going to live?* There was nothing in Fortune Bay or anywhere on Majestic Lake on the luxurious scale to which her father was accustomed.

"Of course you can stay. But where will you sleep? Surely not on the pullout couch."

"The couch will be fine. It won't be for long. I'm looking forward to spending some time with my girl."

She was happy to have him, except for the fact that it would make it pretty well impossible for any quality time alone with Sean—beginning with quashing her hopes for tonight. A year ago she would have been intimidated by the thought of hosting her father in her humble bungalow, but his recent visits had proved he could handle their simpler way of life. Maybe even enjoyed it.

She shot Sean a worried glance. He put a reassuring arm around her shoulders and said to Philip, "It'll be great having you here, we need new blood in the community."

You could always count on Sean to say the right thing, even though Frankie knew that he too must be registering the fact that he'd be going home to his mother and daughter tonight, and every night in the foreseeable future.

Then another thought struck her, and she sucked in a breath. "What about Cookie? You didn't let her go, did you? How will she find another job at her age?"

Her father held up a placating hand. "She's not that old. But no, I didn't let her go. In fact, she's moving out here with me."

Their cook had been like a mother to Frankie ever since her own mother had died when Frankie was five. She'd missed Cookie terribly since she'd moved to Fortune Bay, but despite the closeness, there had always been an unspoken distance between the family and the Help in their household. Although, for many years, there had been a distance between her father and everyone.

"That's great," she said. "But what are you going to *do* here? You're not ready to retire."

"That's the beauty of it," Philip said, his face beaming. "I can do anything I want."

"Like…" Frankie prompted.

"Buy a business, plant a vineyard, buy a couple of planes and run charters. Anything."

Anything was a pretty vague. She just hoped he didn't take too long to figure it out.

Chapter 4

The following morning, Sean was at the office, trying to work in spite of the rhythmic crash and boom of construction down at the shore. He was tweaking the resort's website, still trying to hit just the right tone: family friendly, a fisherman's paradise, but private and up-scale enough for a romantic getaway.

Max had put his heart into the design of the year-round retreat, building a classic lodge with upscale amenities. Giant cedar beams held aloft soaring ceilings in the common rooms and a river rock wall anchored the lobby. The main building was finished and included a restaurant and a bar, reception and admin, and some guest rooms upstairs. One of the separate pods of suites-with-kitchens was finished and there were plans to build more in the forested grounds of the point that stretched into Majestic Lake. Four cottages lined the water on the far side of the point, with more planned for the following year.

Sean was having trouble focusing on his work, his thoughts returning to his argument with Amber and the truncated assignation with Frankie the previous evening. He missed seeing her every day, but was sure she understood that right now, he had to concentrate on getting his daughter settled in her new home.

He'd planned to ask Frankie to marry him and start a family, but when Amber showed up on his doorstep, that had to be put on hold. Amber's upbringing had been rough, and he wanted to offer some moral guidelines—assuming it wasn't already too late. Living with Frankie without being married was not the kind of message he wanted to send to his daughter, especially considering he'd gotten Amber's mother pregnant when they were—*cripes!* —not much older than she was now.

Marrying Frankie was problematic now too, with the animosity Amber showed toward her. Frankie had been nothing but wonderful to his daughter and he could see she was hurt by Amber's constant rebuff. He sighed and turned back to his computer. Just add that to the list of his failures as a father, the first of which had been giving up his daughter in the first place.

When the noise outside suddenly ceased, he heard familiar voices in the lobby. Ready for a break, he walked through the dining room out to the lobby where Max was talking to Frankie and Philip. Max was a tall man, big through the chest, and towered over Frankie's dapper, much smaller father. On his previous visits, Philip had hit it off with Max and last night when Philip had arrived unannounced, he'd told them that Max had been keeping him up to date on local investment opportunities.

After exchanging greetings, Sean left the two

men to talk and taking Frankie's hand, led her outside.

She smiled, but seemed happy to be led. Any few minutes together they could squeeze out of a day were golden. "Where are we going?"

"Here," he said, stopping in the covered entry way and pulling her into his arms. They stood for a moment just holding each other, then he cupped her face in his hands and kissed her deeply, trying to show her he was still there. When he pulled away, she sighed, but not a satisfied sigh, more a frustrated *humph*.

"I know," he said. "We never get any time alone. How long is your father planning to stay?"

Frankie laughed. "Forever, I'm afraid. Not forever with me, but he has no definite plans so it could be a while."

Sean ran a hand through his cropped hair. "And we thought it was hard to find time alone before. Now you're living with your dad and I'm living with my mom and we're sneaking around like some horrible high school flashback. We might have to resort to using the cabin."

Frankie drew a mock-horrified breath. "Is that where you took girls in high school?"

He grinned. "I wish. Aunt Augusta was still living there when I was in high school. No, we had to neck in the car."

He tugged her by the hand down the stone front steps. Cheery groups of daffodils nodded along the front of the covered deck off the dining room. Other bulbs he couldn't name created a misty sea of blue under the trees just beginning to leaf around the parking lot.

"I think the landscaper planned it just right," Sean said. "The Dogwoods should be blooming at Easter for the opening."

"It all looks great. I don't think I've been here since the Christmas party. I drive by every day, but the fir trees screen the buildings and I can't really see anything from the road."

At a sudden barrage of sound, Frankie's eyes widened, and her hands flew up to cover her ears.

"Pile driver," Sean shouted over the noise. "The dock is going in this week. Alex is overseeing the job. He replaced all the docks when he'd bought the marina a couple of years ago, so I offered him the job of putting in the resort docks and helping us buy a few boats for the paying guests to use."

Frankie nodded, hands over her ears. When the noise finally stopped, they followed the path to the shore. After the fire the previous year, Max had hired a crew of gardeners to replant the area with native trees and shrubs. Soon they would grow to soften the edge of the path. Sean often reflected on how Max was single-handedly providing work for half the beleaguered former mill town.

Sean's brother-in-law Alex stood on the shore, his black hair curling out from under his hard hat, a clipboard in one hand and walkie-talkie in the other.

"Almost finished," he said, offering them both

hard hats with noise-muffling ear protectors attached. They put on the gear, Alex gave the signal, and the pile driver went to work. Like a huge industrial crane, it pounded poles into the lakebed to secure the docks. After a few minutes the giant machine ground to a halt, leaving rippling silence in its wake, like rings on the water after a pebble drops into a pond.

A grin on his face, Alex took off his head gear. Sean and Frankie took off theirs as well.

"Looking good," Sean said. "When will all the piles be in?"

"Probably by tomorrow. They've constructed the dock in pieces and will bring it in on Monday," Alex said, still grinning.

A corner of Sean's mouth twitched. "What's tickling you today."

"Colleen's pregnant again."

Sean's smile broadened into a grin. He folded his arms across his chest and rocked back on his heels. "So, my big sister's having another rug rat. Congratulations."

Frankie smiled and shook her head. "I can't believe it. Everyone seems to be getting pregnant. It must be something in the water."

Alex grinned back at Frankie. "You'd better be careful. You could be next."

Frankie laughed. "Maybe I should start drinking bottled water."

Sean shot her a look out of the corner of his eye. *And what exactly did she mean by that?*

Later, back at his desk, Sean's head pounded in time to the noise outside. Had Frankie been serious when she'd told Alex she didn't want to get pregnant? Of course, not right now, not right this minute, but they'd talked about having children together before Amber arrived. Hadn't they? Or had his longing for his daughter been playing tricks on his mind?

He'd have to try to get Frankie alone—although that seemed more impossible every day—and find out exactly what she'd meant, because more children were still in *his* life plan. Just not quite yet.

* * *

Frankie wheeled her Mini Cooper into the Majestic High staff parking lot with minutes to spare. She loved having her father staying with her, but it was playing havoc with her morning routine. Spring showers were the order of the day so, holding her brief case over her head, she raced for the staff entrance.

A throng of milling students filled the hall as she made her way toward her first-period class. She spied Amber leaning against a locker, talking to Derek, the boy Sean had mentioned. He'd been in her composition class the year before, had sat at the back, arms crossed over his brawny chest, never participating in the discussion. With the shadow of a beard along his jaw, he looked older than the other kids. He might have been held back for a year at one point, but he wasn't slow. He'd always handed his work in on time and his stories were creative and well crafted.

Amber flicked her long blonde hair back over her shoulder, exposing one ear, studded with hardware. Derek leaned in and whispered something. Amber giggled in response as Frankie strode by. Such an innocent, girlish sound. Sean was right to be worried.

Frankie walked a fine line with Amber. She couldn't single her out in the hall or the classroom—that would only make her more antagonistic. And Frankie didn't want to rat her out to Sean either. That was no way to win her trust.

When the warning bell sounded, students rolled into the classroom in groups, talking and laughing, in high spirits after their weekend adventures. As they passed her desk, they lay their latest assignments on the corner. The class was reading *Catcher in the Rye* and Frankie had assigned the first three chapters over the weekend and had asked the students to pick out possible themes. A page at most, most of the kids seemed on track. Except for Amber. She shuffled by, head bowed, careful not to catch Frankie's eye. Again, Frankie didn't want to single her out. She was obviously having a hard enough time connecting with the kids in the school—except, apparently, for Derek, who was himself something of an outsider.

When the bell rang to start the period, Frankie

picked up the papers and tapped them against the desk to neaten the pile. "Anyone who was not able to hand in the assignment, please stay and speak to me after class. Now open your books and let's begin."

Forty minutes later, the bell rang again, and the usual commotion ensued as the kids rushed out in a blur of color and noise. Tyler stopped at her desk, obviously embarrassed. "My mom was sick again all weekend. I didn't get it done. I read it though."

Tyler was a good kid, but his home situation was less than stellar. Frankie nodded. "Get it to me tomorrow morning. It doesn't have to be long. Just a few ideas."

In her peripheral vision, she saw Amber hurrying toward the door. "Amber."

The girl stopped in the doorway and turned to face her, tossing back her hair, a defiant look on her face. Frankie came out from behind the desk. She didn't want to pull the authoritarian card, not until she'd tried every other way to get through to the girl.

She smiled. "You seem to be having a bit of trouble getting your work in on time."

Amber looked at the tabletop and mumbled, "I read the book, I just forgot to write the paper."

"It's not even really a paper. I just wanted your thoughts on the emerging themes. What is Holden struggling with? What is he feeling? A few lines are enough for now."

"I'll get it in."

"And I don't have your final paper yet on the short story we read last week."

Amber's eyes flashed up to hers. "I did read that one."

"Good. Well, write up the analysis as I outlined in the assignment handout. Before the end of the week. You don't want to get too far behind."

Amber glanced up and Frankie was surprised to see fear in her eye. "Please, don't tell my father."

Frankie was shocked. Sean would do anything to help Amber. Probably read the darned book for her if she asked. "I won't. There is no need to talk to him about this, yet." She smiled, hoping to diffuse the situation. "Just try to catch up."

"I will." Amber glanced longingly at the door.

"You can go now."

Amber was out the door in a flash, leaving Frankie shaking her head.

Could Amber possibly be afraid of Sean? *Sean?* Hard to believe, but they knew so little about her day-to-day life before she came to live in Fortune Bay, and what they did know was disturbing: drug addicted mother, father not in the picture, abusive alcoholic grandfather. In cases like this, school was often either a refuge or another difficult situation. In Amber's case, Frankie was afraid it had been the latter.

Thinking back, she wondered if Amber's walls had gone up when she discovered Frankie was a teacher at the high school. She had become even more distant since the beginning of this semester when she'd turned up on the role for Frankie's class, but Sean had mentioned other behavioral problems as well, both at home and at school.

Only to be expected, she supposed. But Amber's problems were pushing Frankie and Sean's own plans so far into the distance that she was beginning to wonder if she'd only imagined their future together.

Chapter 5

Max opened the liquor cupboard in Stephanie's kitchen. "Gin & tonic?"

Stephanie smiled. "I'd love one."

She studied the large oil painting standing on the antique sideboard. It was the forest at twilight, all swirls of blue and purple and white, but the colors were not quite right. Too cool. She'd add some soft orange and gold to warm up the composition and to contrast with the cooler colors.

"Thank you," she said as Max set her drink in front of her and settled into a chair at the old oak table.

"And how are things here at the ranch?" he asked.

Stephanie laughed wryly. "It changes day to day. We're kind of on pins and needles, not sure what Amber's going to do next."

The front door opened, and she locked eyes with Max. Muttered curses drifted down the darkened hallway as Sean hung up his coat and kicked off his shoes.

When he entered the kitchen, Stephanie was dismayed to see he looked exhausted.

"Did Amber come home after school," he asked.

"She did," Stephanie was pleased to announce. "She's been up in her room—except for when she came down for dinner. I asked her if she needed any help and she said, no, she was fine. She did ask to see Brandy, but I said she'd have to talk to you about that."

Sean thought for a moment. "I think not. Brandy's a nice girl, but Amber seems to use Brandy as an excuse. I think a week at home is a week at home. It's okay if she watches some television though, once her homework is finished. She's got to get on track with her schoolwork, and missing classes won't help."

"Agreed. Dinner's still on the stove," Stephanie added.

Sean ladled the savory beef stew into a large pottery bowl and cut a hunk of Stephanie's freshly baked bread. While he ate, he and Max discussed the progress at the resort, agreeing that they just might make the Easter opening deadline. When he finished eating, he sat back with a satisfied sigh.

Stephanie smiled. "Better?"

Sean nodded. "Much."

As his mother, Stephanie could see the strain in the lines around his eyes. "Why don't you go out this evening? I'll hold the fort."

A smile softened the worry lines on his forehead. He stood up and touched her arm. "Thanks. I won't be late." Grabbing a jacket off a hook by the back door, he was gone.

Max reached out and covered Stephanie's hand where it lay on the table. "I'll stay for a while."

Stephanie smiled wearily. "I thought we were

past this phase. Last summer when Sean moved out again, I felt like I was finally getting my life on track, learning to be by myself—starting over." She laughed ruefully. "Remember those wonderful, quiet evenings last fall?"

Max smiled broadly. "I certainly do. The house to ourselves. You know you have an open invitation to come over to the farm whenever you can get away?"

Stephanie smiled wanly. "It's a date."

A short time later, Max let himself out the back door, leaving Stephanie's cheeks warm with the burn of his whiskers. She still had a smile on her face when her cell phone rang. Shuffling through the drawings on the table, she found the phone hidden underneath. When she saw her sister Megan's name on the screen, her mood deflated. She huffed out a breath. *Back to reality.*

"Hi, Meg. What's up."

"It's Mother." Megan's high brittle tone told Stephanie they'd been fighting again.

"What is it this time?" Stephanie sat down at the table and rattled the melting ice cubes around in her glass, wishing the drink was still half-full.

"She's impossible. I can't spend my life checking up on her. It's a half hour drive across town each way and she's never glad to see me."

Stephanie snorted a silent laugh. She totally believed that their mother didn't appreciate Megan's visits. Her sister had been bullying their mother for years and she couldn't stand it.

"I don't think she eats. She never has any food

in her fridge."

"Her helper cooks two mornings a week," Stephanie reminded her. "And she has meals delivered two other days. She says the meals are enough for two dinners each. Is she losing weight?"

"Well, no. But she shouldn't be there alone. What if she falls. You hear of elderly people falling all the time. Lying there for hours, even days, in pain before some neighbor notices their newspapers piling up on the doorstep."

Stephanie's conscience prickled at the thought of her mom lying in pain on the bathroom floor. Because of the hour-and-a-half drive each way, Stephanie didn't get to Seattle nearly as often as she'd like and made a mental note to drive in this week and visit her mother. "We could get her to check in by phone every day."

"That won't work. She often doesn't answer her phone."

Not when she knows it's you. "Or set up a phone chain with her neighbors in the condo complex. Some of them must be in the same situation."

"I want her to move into a senior's home. Something closer to me where it will be easier for me to check on her."

"You mean visit her."

"Whatever. There's a facility about a mile away."

"Have you been by to see it?"

"No, but it's probably fine. I called and they

said they had a spot at the end of the month. I told Mom, but she freaked out."

"Maybe you should try asking her."

"We're past asking. She has to move."

"I know you're busy. I'll talk to her. I'll call her tomorrow and try to come to the city this week. Maybe we could set up an appointment to visit the home." She cringed at the term, but the time had come to get more involved. Megan was ten years younger than Stephanie and at fifty, she still had two teenagers at home, as well as a full-time job. Unfortunately, she was the only one of the three siblings still living in Seattle so the burden of overseeing their mother fell on her. And she did consider it a burden.

Stephanie didn't think her mother needed supervision. Yet. She sounded fine during their weekly phone calls, but she was well into her eighties and living alone. Maybe she would like to move somewhere where she had more company and someone to prepare her meals. But Dorothy was feisty. It had to be her decision and on her terms.

"I don't have time to run around checking on every little thing," Megan said.

"I'll go and see her. I'll try to get her to go and look at the place with me."

"Good luck. She'll never agree."

"Leave it to me. We'll talk later."

They hung up and Stephanie punched in her mother's number. It rang until it went to voice mail. "Hi, Mom. Call me when you get this. Or—

I'll call you tomorrow." She hung up, laid her phone on the table and stared at it. Her mother only had a land line so she wouldn't answer if she wasn't home. She was probably at bingo at the senior's center. She'd try her again in the morning.

Stephanie heaved a dramatic sigh. She felt squeezed on one side by her sister and mother and on the other by her son and teenage grandchild, like a sandwich, with her as the filling. Her sister had two teenagers and a husband at home, so she must feel the same way. No wonder she was so crabby all the time.

Making herself a cup of herbal tea, she sat at the table again and wished she could have gone home with Max tonight. She hadn't realized how much she'd come to value his company until it became hard to get. Maybe if Sean didn't get home too late, she'd head over to Max's for some quiet time later. He'd said to come any time.

She ran her eye over the painting leaning against the kitchen wall. Maybe a spark of spring green would brighten up the purple shadows.

Chapter 6

Sean stood on the back steps of his mother's house and took a deep, revitalizing breath. The air smelled like spring, wet winter moss and life stirring in the ground. If he stood very still, he could hear the high chirping of the frog chorus in the marsh across the road. A definite sign of spring.

The days were getting longer and even now, with the sun sinking behind the mountain across the lake, there was still light in the sky. He welcomed the energetic quality in the breeze blowing in, carrying with it the scent of lake and evergreens. He'd walk to Frankie's. It was only ten minutes along the lakeside path but over the winter he'd got out of the habit of walking. December had been unusually cold but bright, a solid month of sparkling ice and a dusting of crusty snow on the ground. January had been warmer, but the rains had set in.

Tonight, though, the weather was fine and as he walked, he thought over his impasse with Amber. Why couldn't she work with him? This was a great opportunity for her—a new home, a new chance. It had to be better than what she'd left behind, didn't it? Otherwise why would she have run away to find him? Sean had filed for legal custody right away and her grandfather, Jasper, a nasty drunk who fate had made her legal guardian, didn't seem to be fighting it. Probably thought it was too much trouble.

So why wasn't she happy? Wasn't this what she wanted? Teenage girls were a mystery. He just hoped she wasn't a victim of the same hormones that had ruled her mother's life at that age. And his.

Of course she is. And probably confused to boot. At first he'd been lenient, giving her space, but she needed to know his expectations. She might not be college bound, that wasn't for everyone, but she had to go to class and finish high school. That was non-negotiable.

He came out of the woods into the large clearing where the path ran along a small beach in front of his brother Jake's new, yellow farmhouse. In the gathering dusk, lights shone from the first-floor windows. Last fall, when Amber and Frankie had come into his life, Sean had thought he was on the road to having what Jake had, a home and a family. But that wasn't working out as neatly as he'd planned.

He followed the path along the shore, back into the trees to the cabin his mother owned. It was dark and empty now, but he'd lived there last summer for a few idyllic months. That's when he'd really gotten to know Frankie.

He stopped at the cabin steps. It was a well-known fact among the Murphy family that the companionable spirit of his great-aunt Augusta still inhabited the cabin. He hoped she wasn't too lonely. She seemed to like company—or at least, she liked to interfere in her tenant's lives. He smiled to remember how instrumental she had been in bringing him and Frankie together.

He climbed the steps to the porch and sat in the gathering dusk on the faded old couch and stared out at the lake. An almost-full moon rose above the mountain, laying a bright path of moonlight across the still water. He sat back and folded his arms on his chest.

Although he'd been plagued by thoughts of finding Amber, he'd enjoyed the carefree months he'd spent in the cabin. Frankie was excitingly different than the other women he knew in Fortune Bay. He'd dated most of them when he was growing up and hadn't expected to find someone new when he'd returned to Fortune Bay three years ago for his father's funeral. She'd been resistant, he smiled to remember, but he'd been persistent and finally won her over.

He'd been looking for Amber, and when the official search channels dried up and he almost gave up hope, Frankie had encouraged him to continue the search. Then just when he had decided to ask her to marry him, he'd found his daughter.

Hard as it was to build a relationship with Amber—and heaven knows, they still had a long way to go—he'd never give her up now. But for some reason, Amber didn't seem to like Frankie, and he didn't know how to fix that. He had put his marriage plans on hold and thought Frankie would understand, but she seemed to grow more distant every day. He had to figure out how to turn things around.

A warm breeze shifted the air on the porch, like the back of a hand brushing his cheek.

"That you, Augusta?" he murmured. "I know, it's time to pick things up with Frankie again."

As he thought back to those early days together, he felt the need stir again. "But first I have to figure out what to do about Amber."

He'd been separated from his daughter for half his life and all through those years, the thought of her out there, somewhere, had held him hostage. Finding her had been liberating—at first. But now he could feel the bonds of worry and failure tighten around him again. He couldn't go back to living like that. He had to make a move. He'd just have to make Amber see how living with Frankie would be good for them all.

With renewed energy, he stood up, patting the porch post on his way by. "Thanks for the pep talk, Augusta."

He followed the path through the fringe of mature fir trees to Frankie's yard and climbed the stairs to her back deck, the glow from her living room windows lighting his way.

* * *

Frankie was curled up on the couch reading

when she heard a knock on the patio door. The door slid opened and Sean's head poked through, his blonde eyebrows raised in question.

Frankie's pulse quickened and she rose to meet him. "Dad's out."

Sean stepped inside, kicked off his boots and met her halfway. With a devilish smile, he pulled her to him and kissed her thoroughly. His hands pressed her against him until she felt his warmth in all the right places, and she softened into the kiss.

They were still fine. When they were alone together and she had his full attention, they were still fine. This was exactly what she needed, and she wasn't getting nearly enough of it these days.

When they came up for air, he leaned his forehead against hers. "Hello."

She smiled. "Hello." Taking his hand, she led him to the couch. He looked wistfully down the hall to the bedroom. "How long is your dad going to be out?"

She laughed and tugged his hand to pull him down beside her. "What is this, a booty call?"

He had the grace to look chagrined. "No. But I do miss seeing you, being with you every day. We don't have nearly enough quality time together lately."

She leaned her head against his shoulder. "I know. I miss seeing you every evening. I miss having dinner together every night."

He kissed her temple. "That too."

She laughed and moaned with a sadness that

was only half-feigned. "And it's only gotten worse since my dad got here. There has to be a way we can find more time together."

He grinned. "There's always the cabin."

She punched him gently in the arm. "I'm being serious here—"

"So am I—"

"Last fall you said the cabin was too cold." She nestled back into the crook of his arm, loving his solid warmth beside her. "I'd love to be living together again."

Sean straightened slightly, his arm slipping off her shoulder, and gave her a gentle smile. "We were never officially living together."

Frankie blinked. That stung. Maybe not officially, but before Amber had shown up unannounced, he had insinuated himself pretty snuggly into her house and her life. Sure, initially she'd been helpless after her accident, but he'd been wonderful, taking care of her like that. And, over time, they'd grown close.

Very close. She'd thought it was more than just proximity. Everyone had thought that. They were way beyond the toothbrush stage. Her friends had a field day teasing her as more and more of his stuff migrated into her small bungalow. Most of it was still here. All that was missing was him.

"Maybe not officially, but I thought we were heading in that direction."

"I did too. I still do. But Amber has complicated everything."

"I know, but—"

He shook his head. "She's still so moody and unstable."

"She's a teenage girl."

"I know, but I have to cut her some slack. You know how awful her home life was before she ran away. Never seeing her mom."

"Which was probably a good thing since she was a drug addict, living in a biker house."

"I agree. But she's never had a good role model and I really want to be that for her. I want *us* to be that. Shacking up together would send the wrong message."

Frankie pulled away sharply. "We wouldn't be shacking up."

Sean put a soothing hand on her shoulder, but she refused to be placated. "I know. We are both solid and working and not addicts but, call me old fashioned, I'd like to give her a real family."

She sensed a 'but.' "But not with me."

"Yes, with you," he said with feeling. "But there's a lot to think about. A lot to straighten out first. We'd have to find a place big enough for us all to live in and, to be honest, for some reason, you are not Amber's favorite person."

He tried to soften his words by rubbing her shoulder, but Frankie's cheeks burned. "I have tried—"

"I know you have. I don't know what the problem is. Maybe she's jealous, or worried you don't want her—"

"I've never given her any reason to think that."

"I know. Who understands how teenagers think?"

I should, Frankie thought, a frown wrinkling her forehead.

"I'll work on that," he said, nuzzling her temple. "Once the resort opens, I'll have more time."

The resort. These days, it always came first. Then Amber. Or the other way around. Either way, Frankie was last on the list.

She got it. He was busy. The job at the resort was a wonderful opportunity for him. But they'd only been together a few months before Amber arrived and Sean got the new job, and sometimes she worried they hadn't been together long enough to build a strong enough foundation to make it through this tough time.

Her sigh deflated the rod stiffening her spine. "I'll try to think of something to do with Amber that will be fun." *Other than fail her in English.*

He was silent for a moment. "The school phoned. She's been skipping classes."

Frankie's mind went straight to their confrontation in the classroom. "Today?"

"Today and other days. She can't seem to keep up with the workload. Is that common when kids switch schools?"

She frowned as she considered the question. "I don't know what the standards were like at the other school, what the workload was and what her marks were like."

"None of us really know."

"And she didn't just switch schools, she switched in mid-semester. That can be tough. But we're into a new semester now and she should be starting to settle in."

"How is she doing in your class?"

She pressed her lips together. She had promised Amber she wouldn't rat her out to Sean, but now that he'd specifically asked, wasn't it better to be proactive? Better to step in before Amber got any farther behind?

"I'm afraid she is falling behind in the work. Maybe if you spent a bit of time with her, asked her about what we're studying. Right now, we're reading and analyzing *Catcher in the Rye*."

"I can't do her homework for her."

"I'm not asking you to. Just to be a little more involved." She mentally slapped her forehead. *That came out wrong.*

Sean stood up abruptly, leaving her reeling on the sofa. He was seething.

"Sean—"

The front door flew open and they both turned to look. Philip stood on the threshold, looking pleased as punch. "You won't believe what I bought today."

Sean grabbed his jacket. "Sorry, Philip, I've got to go." And he stormed out the door.

Chapter 7

Sean started along the path at a brisk pace. An angry pace. He was angry at Amber for being so darn uncooperative, and angry at Frankie for suggesting he wasn't doing enough as a parent.

Having grown up in Fortune Bay, he knew every root and hollow of the shoreline path, even in the dark and his pace didn't slow until he approached his mother's house. Stopping in the open backyard, he looked at the moon hanging over the mountain across the lake. An eternity of stars filled the sky.

How was he supposed to know how to handle this situation? He'd had no warmup to being a father and certainly had no experience. His lack of parenting experience wasn't Frankie's fault, but she could be more understanding. Couldn't she see he was doing his best? Obviously, it wasn't good enough if Amber was having trouble at school. If she needed help, he didn't know how to give it if she wouldn't let him in. But one thing he did know, getting angry was just pushing both Amber and Frankie away.

How long had it been since he'd gotten out his telescope? Months. Not since he'd done that stargazing with Frankie last fall. Looking at the heavens always put his life into perspective. Amber might even think was cool. He frowned.

Maybe not. He didn't have a clue what she thought.

He headed into the house, wishing, not for the first time, that teenagers came with a book of instructions.

Kicking off his shoes in the back sunporch, Sean let himself into the house. His mother was sitting in her kitchen armchair contemplating the bold abstract painting that still stood on the sideboard. She turned to him and smiled expectantly, eyebrows raised.

He shook his head and dropped into one of the straight-back chairs. "Frankie says Amber's falling behind in her schoolwork."

Stephanie tilted her head. "Did she have any suggestions?"

Anger boiled up to the surface again. "She said I should get more involved. But how? I've turned my life upside down for that girl."

Stephanie glanced down the hall and put her finger to her lips. He lowered his voice. "Doesn't she like it here? I don't know what more I can do."

"Maybe you should talk to her."

"I've tried."

Stephanie smiled. "Try again. Did Frankie say anything else?"

Sean ran a hand over his chin and rested it on his neck. "Not really. Just that she's feeling left out. Surely she understands that our plans have to be on hold for a while?"

"Did you have plans, together?" Stephanie asked mildly.

"I had plans." He looked at the floor. "I don't know if she actually knew about them. I felt uncomfortable discussing them while I was still looking for Amber, didn't think it was fair to Frankie when my life was such a mess. Then suddenly Amber was on the scene and pow, everything changed. But as long as Amber has this," he shook his head, searching for the word, "*animosity* toward Frankie, we can't move forward. I don't know what to do."

"Why don't you go and talk to Louise. She seems to have forged a bond with Amber. In fact, I'd go so far as to say, Amber worships her."

He nodded. "I haven't seen Amber as excited about anything as she was about helping Louise bake for the Christmas show at the resort."

"Louise has probably spent as much time with her as anyone—except maybe Brandy. She might have some insight."

"Good idea."

"But not tonight. It's my turn to go out." Stephanie stood up, grabbed her poncho off the hook and her car keys from the blown glass bowl on the sideboard. "Sounds like you have a lot to think about. I'm going over to Max's for a while."

Sean nodded as his mother swept out of the room.

He grabbed a beer from the fridge and sat down to enjoy it in his mother's chair. Didn't he deserve a life too? Amber's arrival and the job had swept his own plans under the rug. It had always been too easy for him to immerse himself in other people's problems at the cost of moving forward in his own life. He frowned. Or was it to *avoid* moving his own life forward?

He'd had a plan and it had felt damn good. He would start looking for a house, or property to build one, again first thing tomorrow. He couldn't let Frankie and his dream of a family drift away.

* * *

Stephanie pulled up outside the old log house. Except for the light leaking out around the living room blind, you wouldn't have known that anyone was home. The farmhouse belonged to her, but Max had been renting it for the past nine months, so when she stepped up on the low veranda, she knocked on the heavy wood door.

Sean's mood when he came home from Frankie's had been almost as bad as when he'd gone. This situation must be taking a toll on their relationship. Too bad. Things had been looking so good for him a few months ago.

Stephanie hoped he didn't think he had to choose between Frankie and Amber. Sean tended to put the needs of others ahead of his own. His caring nature was one of his most appealing qualities, but as his mother, she'd like to see him, just once, put his own needs first.

She agreed with him that one of them should try to be home whenever Amber was there—or was supposed to be there—but sometimes the tension was wearing. The farm had become Stephanie's oasis for adult time since Amber had moved in. Sometimes she wished she could stay with Max all night, but she rarely did.

Max opened the heavy wooden door and beamed a welcoming smile when he saw it was her.

"Is this a good 'any time'?" she asked.

He took her hand and pulled her inside. When he put his arms around her, she felt the tension go out of her shoulders.

"Glass of wine?" he asked.

"Oh, yes."

He chuckled.

"You can laugh," she said, following him into the kitchen. "Living alone in this peaceful oasis."

"Sometimes it's too peaceful. I get lonely."

She laughed wryly. "Be careful what you wish for."

"You know I want us to live together."

Stephanie pressed her lips together pensively. "And you know I need some time living alone. I've never lived alone—except for that sliver of time between when Sean moved out last summer and moved back in again last fall. I was just getting into a rhythm, figuring out who I am—besides a mother, a grandmother and a wife. It wasn't long enough. I need more time."

They'd been over this before and she'd hoped he'd understood. He'd thought his divorce would make a difference to her, and it had. It meant that they could spend time together as a couple—but it hadn't changed her desire to live alone for a while.

"Whereas I've been living virtually alone for twenty years." He sighed. "I guess I can wait a few more."

He handed her the glass of wine he'd poured, and she rewarded him, for the wine and understanding, with a solid, heartfelt kiss. Then they went into the living room.

It had taken a few months for Max to settle in at the farm. At first, he'd made do with the furniture Jake had left behind when he moved out, basic bachelor décor. But just before Christmas, in one fell swoop, Max had furnished the entire living room. To Stephanie's eye, the brown leather couch and chair and the dark wood end table and coffee table set, looked like it came straight off a showroom floor. It probably had, but he was happy. She'd helped him pick out a few bright cushions and gave him a large colorful landscape of her own that he had admired. With some soft lighting, the room had become an inviting escape, especially because it was also quiet and devoid of people.

He settled beside her on the couch, sliding one arm around her shoulders along the back. They'd get to that, but he seemed to understand that first she needed to unwind.

"Did you work things out at home?" he asked.

"For now. Amber seems to be struggling at school. I think she needs more than Sean and I just telling her to do the work. I don't know what, though. It may be as simple as learning good study habits. And then there's the boyfriend."

"He seems to be a bad influence."

Stephanie laughed. "As the mother of two sons, I'd say they're *all* bad influences. I don't know if he's any worse than most." She shook her head. "Let's just make this a kid free zone. Or at least a kid free night."

Max pulled her close and kissed her neck. "Can you stay all night? I have a lovely quiet bed upstairs, and I would sneak out in the morning and let you sleep."

"Sounds tempting, but I should probably go home at some point." His kisses burned along her neck, and her resistance began to soften like chocolate. Would it hurt to spend the odd night together? Surely everyone would get used to the idea eventually.

"You don't have to decide now, but let's not waste the time we have." Max stood up, pulled her to her feet and nudged her toward the staircase. She waited on the bottom step while he made a quick detour into the kitchen to top up their glasses then, laughing, they started up the stairs together.

They were halfway up when someone knocked on the front door. Stephanie groaned and turned to face him.

"Let's not answer it," he whispered.

She shook her head. "We have to."

"I'll make it quick." He handed her the wine glasses and hurried down the stairs. Flicking on the outside light, he swung open the door.

A woman stood on the porch. She looked to be in her mid-thirties, stringy shoulder-length hair pulled behind her ears, her eyes too big, her face pale in the harsh overhead light.

She looked tearfully at Max. "Hi, Daddy."

"Lily." Max appeared to be in shock. He just stood there, holding open the door, not asking her in. She glanced to the side, as if assessing her escape, and that seemed to push his start button. "Honey, what are you doing here? Come in."

He stepped back and she grabbed her rolling suitcase and stepped inside. They stood in the foyer, just looking at each other. Neither seemed to know how to begin.

Stephanie started down the stairs. "You must be Lily. Max has told me so much about you."

Max turned and stared at Stephanie as if he'd forgotten she was there. *Men.* "I'm Stephanie. Nice to finally meet you." She put the glasses of wine on the hall table and gave the girl a gentle hug. Anything more and the girl might shatter.

Lily's eyes locked on the wine glasses, then widened. "I'm interrupting." Her cheeks turned red.

"No, no," Stephanie said. She glanced at Max. *Jump in any time.* "We were just having a drink. Would you like a glass of wine?"

Lily bit her lip and looked at Max. Stephanie gave him an elbow in the ribs.

"Yes. Let me get you a drink." Max picked up their glasses and hustled into the kitchen.

"Okay." Lilly blew out a shaky breath and followed.

Stephanie pulled out a chair at the table. "Come and sit." In her experience, the kitchen was the place for family meetings. She knew Max's relationship with his daughter wasn't close, that he'd been afraid of losing touch completely after his divorce, but with a bit of urging he had called her at Christmas. Now that she saw them together, Stephanie realized their relationship was worse than she had thought.

Max set their glasses down on the kitchen table and a moment later returned with a third. "I don't know. Is red okay?"

"Yes. Of course."

Stephanie pursed her lips in exasperation. They were being too darned polite. But once he sat with them at the table, Max seemed able to take charge. "So, Lily, what's going on?"

She took a deep breath and blew it out. "I left Troy."

Max was silent for a moment, then nodded. "I didn't know you were having trouble."

Lilly looked at the table and shook her head. She didn't seem to know where to start. When she looked up, tears glistened in her eyes. "Can I stay here with you for a while?"

Before long, Stephanie said goodbye. Max needed time to catch up with his daughter and from the looks of thing, that could take a while.

He walked her to the door and out onto the porch. The night was clear, the air crisp. He shoved his hands deep into his pockets and his shoulders hunched forward. "Sorry." He gave her a sheepish grin. "Not the evening I was hoping for."

"I understand." She smiled and tightened her scarf. "So, Lily."

He pressed his lips together and nodded. "Yes, Lily. I've hardly seen her since she went off to college. That was almost twenty years ago. Of course, I went to her wedding, but I was on the road so darn much for work, I relied on her mother to keep us in touch. Now that Marion and I are divorced, I've been trying to rekindle the relationship, but it's been hard. We've drifted so far apart."

"Interesting she decided to come here now."

"She's left her husband. I guess she's looking for a place to hide."

Stephanie frowned. "Is he abusive?"

Max looked thoughtful for a moment, then shook his head. "I don't think so. I don't know what the problem is. It must have been pretty spur of the moment or she would have called."

"Maybe she was afraid you'd say no."

He looked shocked. "I hope not. I welcome the chance to help her, to make up for all those lost years."

"I understand," Stephanie repeated, and kissed him on the cheek. "Go inside and talk to your daughter."

She felt his eyes on her as she walked to her car.

Another oasis gone, she thought as she drove down the gravel drive, the lights of the farmhouse turning into starry specs in the rearview mirror. Too late to drop in on another friend, she took the road home instead.

Oh, well. What can you do? Family trumps romance, at least for tonight.

Chapter 8

The following morning, Sean was trying to concentrate on the press release he was supposed to be writing as a follow-up to their grand opening. He knew he'd be too busy to write it after the opening and would be glad to have these pieces ready to go. Instead, though, his mind was on the scene with Amber when he'd suggested, in a perfectly reasonable tone of voice, that she might need a tutor if the work at school was too challenging.

He'd thought it out beforehand and was careful to say *challenging,* not too hard or too difficult, but she still exploded, said she could do the work on her own. Then she'd stormed out of the house in storm trooper boots, black tights, a short, frilly, black-lace skirt and a long, baggy grey sweater that might have been a hand-me-down from her grandmother. Once, he'd suggested that they go shopping for new clothes. He would never do *that* again. She had been mortified by the suggestion. He just wanted to buy her something nice, make her happy, make her life easier, but she took everything he said as criticism.

And where had she gotten that from, he thought with chagrin as he remembered exploding at Frankie the night before when she suggested Amber might need more help with her schoolwork than he'd been giving her. Than she'd *let* him give her, he'd wanted to point out. He'd have to apologize to Frankie for that, although he did feel she could have been more diplomatic in her delivery.

Mindlessly tapping a pencil on the desk, he stared out the window. The forest understory was a haze of green buds and unfurling leaves. Like white froth, the first native shrubs had burst into bloom; a cascade of tiny Ocean Spray blossoms and the stiff upright blooms of the Red Elderberry. Through it, he caught glimpses of sunlight sparkling on the lake. What he wouldn't give to be out on the lake in his boat, fishing line in the water, all his cares left behind. But even that probably wouldn't wipe away his worries today.

He gave his head a shake. He wasn't going to get anything done here at work until he devised a strategy for his future, and that meant, first, helping Amber get settled. He just had to look at it like a business problem and come up with an approach that would solve the conflict and get his life plan back on track.

First, he'd take his mother's advice and talk to Louise. She seemed to have the best relationship with Amber, seemed to know how to talk to the girl without getting her back up. Maybe she'd have some idea of an approach to take.

In the parking lot, the breeze off the water lifted his spirits. Breathing deeply, he blew out a breath, releasing some of his pent-up anxiety about

Amber and Frankie and the grand opening coming up. To be honest, though, work was the least stressful part of his life these days. Maybe he had buried himself at the resort lately because it was easier than dealing with Amber and his guilt about not spending enough time with Frankie.

Climbing into his low red Miata, he spun out of the parking lot. Amber wasn't quite the golden-haired darling he'd been expecting when he'd gone looking for his daughter, and he could see now that his thoughts had been unrealistically simplistic about the happy family they would morph into when they met. He had felt an immediate spark when he first saw her, and love had washed over him like a giant wave, infusing every pore of his body. But as the weeks and months rolled by, although the love had grown, reality had set in, overwhelming him with a sense of responsibility, and inadequacy, as he began to see the extent of her problems.

It was only to be expected with her tough upbringing. He could see that in some ways she was trying hard to fit into the family. Her swearing had all but disappeared as she sensed it was unacceptable. His mother had made that clear in her firm-but-gentle way. Sean didn't feel he was getting through to Amber though, didn't even know if she believed he loved her and wanted her to be there.

Gravel crunched under his tires as he wheeled into Blue and Louise's driveway. Blue had bought the log house the previous autumn, and luckily, had spread that load of gravel or Sean's low-slung car would have bellied out in the potholes. He could see that Blue had already started the porch that would eventually wrap around the house. Where it faced the lake, the sitting area would be wide enough for a small table and a couple of chairs. Their location on the point allowed a one-hundred-and-eighty-degree view of the water. It was one of the prime lots on the shore. Lakefront was at a premium with most of the lake bound up in forestry contracts and the National Park, and Sean knew he was unlikely to find anything nearly as good.

He rapped on the door and let himself in. Louise called out a greeting and he followed her voice around the corner into the new kitchen Blue had built for her. She was rolling out dough on the marble island, looking round and radiant, like a Madonna.

Sean had known her all his life, and the sight brought him to a halt. "What-cha making?"

"Freezer pies, for the resort. Just stocking up. I won't bake them until we need them. I've been thinking, we should give the dining room a name. We've called the bar 'the Cedars', and I think we need a name for the dining room, too. After all, it's not just the guests who will be coming there to eat. Maybe something to do with the swimming salmon Blue carved around the doorway."

"Good idea. I'll mention it to Max. Do you have time for a bit of a break?"

"Sure. Any excuse to get off my feet. Put on the kettle."

While Sean waited for the kettle to boil, bands of anxiety tightened around his chest. He was probably overly defensive. Talking about Amber's problems was difficult, but that wasn't getting him—any of them—anywhere.

They settled in the living room and he searched his mind for a place to start.

Louise stretched her back. "I'm so glad to have Amber and Brandy lined up to help me in the kitchen this summer. With the babies coming, I'm going to need it. But a job like this right here in town was too good an opportunity to pass up."

Sean straightened up. "Amber loves working with you. I'd almost say it's the thing she loves to do most."

Louise nodded. "She's a natural. You only need to show her something once. She seems to memorize the recipes the first time she makes them. Brandy is a good kitchen helper too, but I think she'll turn out to be a better babysitter than pastry chef. At least for now, until she figures out what she wants to do with her life. I've confirmed things with Max, and we're going to keep the menu simple to start. That's why I'm putting these pies in the freezer at the resort. By the time these babies are ready to pop, I'm confident Amber will be able to handle the breakfast baking and simple deserts for a few weeks without me." She laughed. "I warned her it means getting up really early most mornings, but she didn't seem to care."

"That's what confuses me," Sean said cautiously. "She's willing to go above and beyond to work with you, but she's really struggling with school."

"School's not for everyone," Louise said.

"I know. I don't necessarily expect her to go to college, but I really want her to finish high school."

"Is that in doubt?"

"Frankie says she's failing her English class, not handing in work, sometimes not even showing up for classes."

Louise leaned back on the couch. "That must be hard on Frankie. She already seems to be having trouble connecting with Amber. Having to be a disciplinarian will only make it worse."

"I'm having the same problem. I want to build a bond with her, but instead I seem to be yelling at her all the time." He shook his head. "Usually, I can handle people. It's what I do best. But I'm totally confused about Amber. I don't know what to do. The school's been calling, saying she's skipping classes."

Louise's forehead wrinkled in thought. "That's not good, but yelling's certainly not the way to go."

"I just feel angry all the time. Probably at myself, really, but I'm taking it out on Amber and Frankie, and even my mother, who has been nothing but a rock through all this." He looked morosely at the floor.

"Don't beat yourself up. This is a huge adjustment for both you and Amber. Any teenager would have trouble adjusting, but Amber's also just lost her mother and grandmother. She's probably still mourning. You know how long it to me to process my mother's death. Years."

"You're right." He sat up and thumped the heel of his palm on his forehead. "I'm an idiot. I haven't been factoring that in."

"We need to do something to lighten the mood," Louise said, tapping a finger on her chin. "Something totally unrelated to school. Let's have a games night this weekend. Just you and Frankie, Amber and Brandy, and Blue and me. It'll be fun. Maybe Amber can come over in the afternoon and help me make some goodies. I'm not promising anything, but maybe I can get her to talk to me about the situation at school."

Sean's shoulders relaxed for the first time in days. "That would be terrific. A fun family night. It's exactly what we need."

Chapter 9

Students bounded in packs out of Frankie's classroom. Amber should have been with them, but she hadn't shown up for class. Frankie was angry and concerned and uncertain in turns about how to proceed. She had to mark her absent—didn't she? She couldn't let her personal relationship with Amber—and Sean—get in the way of her job. It wasn't like at the café when Louise used to slip a free donut the firemen after a blaze. This was a case of professional ethics and she wouldn't be able face herself if she bent the rules for Amber.

She sensed Amber's behavior was more than just acting out. Something was bothering the girl and professional ethics demanded she get to the bottom of it, not just mark her absent and write her off. But what would marking her absent really accomplish? She leaned back against the desk, one arm across her chest the other fist pressed to her lips, weighing the pros and cons of each possible action.

She would let it go for today, but she would try to get to the root of the problem.

Her professional watchdog satisfied, she marked Amber present and headed down the hall to Matthew Swallow's science classroom, thinking he might have Amber in his Biology 10 class this year.

Frankie tapped on his door and stuck her head into the room. "Got a moment?"

Matthew was peering into a microscope. He straightened his lanky frame at the intrusion and beamed when he saw her. "Frankie, hi. What can I do for you?"

Matthew was a nice guy, and for a moment last summer Frankie had wondered if they could have been more than casual friends. She had quickly decided they couldn't, but thankfully, they'd remained friends.

"Do you have Amber Murphy, in your class?"

Matthew's bushy eyebrows came together in a frown. "I have her this semester."

A worrying response. Frankie's heart clutched. "How is she doing? Is she keeping up with the assignments? I'm a little worried about her. Did you know she's Sean's daughter?"

Matthew pressed his lips together. He knew about Frankie and Sean's relationship, but possibly didn't know Sean was Amber's father.

"I didn't. I only knew she was a transfer student, so I was prepared to give her a little extra TLC, you know, extra time on assignments or help after class, but she's got to meet me half way."

"What do you mean?"

"She is not handing in assignments and her lab reports are barely legible."

Relief rushed through her. *It's not only me.* Frankie pressed her lips together and nodded, not sure if she should welcome the feeling. "That's what I feared." *Or hoped. No feared. Definitely feared.*

Amber obviously had a wide-ranging problem, which was bad. But it meant her absences weren't directed at Frankie, and that would be good. But Frankie was still Amber's teacher and would eventually have to give her a grade. Then it could easily become personal.

She thanked Matthew for his feedback and went down to the office. After slipping her attendance sheets through the slot in the counter, she hesitated.

"Can I help you," Marjory, the office secretary asked without looking up from her monitor.

"Yes," Frankie said, suddenly sure of what she needed to do. "A new student transferred in last term. May I see her transcript?"

Marjorie swiveled and opened the bottom desk drawer. "Name?"

"Amber Fallow. Or Murphy. She was Fallow when she transferred."

Marjorie slapped the file on the counter. "Don't take it out of the room." Then, thankfully, she showed no interest in why Frankie wanted to see the papers and returned to her computer screen.

Frankie took the folder over to a chair in the corner beside a small table. Ruffling through the reports inside, she saw that Amber's marks had always been abysmally low. The previous year she had barely scraped through, receiving mostly D's in academic subjects, a B in Home Ec, and C's in Gym. Looking back to other years, she saw she occasionally pulled off a C in math, and got straight A's across the board in art.

Thoughtfully, Frankie closed the folder. What did it mean? Amber wasn't dumb. Although withdrawn, she could speak intelligently on certain subjects. She talked basketball with Sean and while not Frankie's thing, Sean said Amber's recall of players' numbers and plays was quite phenomenal.

Frankie felt excitement rise in her chest. She'd have to give this a little more thought and take a careful look at Amber's assignments, but she had an idea of what might be the problem. And if she was right, the discovery could be just what they needed to get all their lives back on track, before things went too far and she lost Sean forever.

* * *

Stephanie clutched the neck of the bottle through the crinkled paper bag and tapped on the big front door of the resort lobby. Through the glass she could see that the dimly lit lobby was empty.

The evening was chilly, and she pulled her jacket closer to her neck. The silk blouse she wore underneath had no warmth, but she'd made an effort to dress up tonight. Glancing back over her shoulder, she saw Max's old Jag was the only other car in the lot. *The Cedars* bar wasn't open and for once Sean had gone home tonight at a reasonable time.

That's when Max had called to say they'd have the resort to themselves.

With Lily at his house and Sean and Amber at hers, they'd had to get creative. This sneaking around to have a quiet meeting—let's face it, she thought with a chuckle, to have sex—made the evening even more exciting. She could see why some couples got into role playing—not that she wanted anything kinky—for her, getting out of her painting clothes was enough of a thrill—but the air of intrigue certainly livened things up.

She rapped again, this time more loudly. Max hurried out of his office behind the reception desk and walked through the dimly lit lobby to unlock the big glass door for her. He'd taken off his suitcoat, loosened his tie, unbuttoned the top button of his shirt and rolled up his sleeves. She'd been married to a logger for thirty-five years and found Max's shirt-and-tie thing novel and very sexy. His thick salt-and-pepper hair was a little longer than usual and slightly mussed, as if he'd been running his fingers through it while he worked. Her fingers clenched. She wanted to run her fingers through it, too.

His normally serious expression lightened into a smile as he let her in and relocked the door. She put one hand against his chest, on the crisp white shirt. He pressed her back against the door and cradled her face between his hands, taking his time with the kiss, letting her know he'd been waiting for her and thinking about their plan for an evening of love in one of the rooms upstairs.

She melted against him. She was tall, but he was taller, and with his broad shoulders and strong arms, he made her feel like a girl again.

The bottle in the paper bag clunked against the wall as she wrestled off her jacket and threw it on the reception desk. He undid the top pearl button of her silk blouse and kissed the cleavage that rose above her lacy bra, making her glad she'd gone to the trouble of dressing up.

They kissed as they stumbled around the lobby to darkened hall in front of the elevators. Impatiently, Max pressed the call button behind her back and went back to devouring her neck. She couldn't wait to get up to the room so she could put down the bottle and join in more fully, but this was pretty darn good for now.

Her hair disheveled and cheeks burning from his five o'clock shadow, she undid another button on his shirt and slid her hand inside, feeling his warm, hard chest, lightly covered with springy hair, and his pounding heart. They might not make it up to the room after all.

The front door swung open. "Mom?" Sean's voice rose to a surprised tenor.

Max froze, his lips plastered to hers. His eyes flew open, an inch from her own. Then he took a step back. Stephanie blinked slowly, as the blood that just a minute ago had been hot and rushing through her veins turned cold and sluggish and seemed to sink into her feet, pinning her to the floor.

Sean was holding a big, round pane of glass, the diameter equal to the spread of his arms. He leaned it against the reception desk and turned to open the door again, glancing back at them over his shoulder as Jake and Blue muscled in a big, burly chunk of wood.

Stephanie leaned against the wall behind Max as she fumbled to do up the buttons of her blouse. *Damn!* Then she stepped out to greet her sons.

Jake stepped back to leave the final placement of the piece to Blue and suddenly realized what they'd walked in on. His jaw dropped and his eyes shifted, his gaze connecting with Sean's. Blue seemed unaware of everyone else as he rolled the root ball into place. While the Murphy's all stared at one another, apparently unable to move, Max hurried over and helped Blue lift the glass into place. With the addition of the glass top, the root ball suddenly became a sculptural table base, the perfect centerpiece for the lobby.

Max turned to Sean, the stern look back on his face. "You're back. I thought you were gone for the night."

Obviously. Stephanie held back a chuckle as she patted her hair into place.

"Just making a delivery," Sean said, looking his boss straight in the eye. A muscle twitched in his jaw, but he managed not to crack a smile.

Stephanie stepped forward to study the table,

inching her way around it toward the front door. "It's gorgeous, Blue."

Blue brushed an infinitesimal speck of dust off the top and mumbled, "Thanks."

"You've outdone yourself, don't you think, Max?"

Max looked a little surprised. "Yes. Great job." He finally found his feet and came around to join her, grabbing her jacket from the reception desk on his way by.

"Ready to go?" she said briskly.

Max held the door open for her. "Ready when you are."

"Night, boys," she said and walked boldly out the door and down the front steps.

As they walked to their cars, Stephanie collapsing against Max in laughter. "*That* was awkward. I feel like a teenager, caught in the act."

"It was perfect." Max said gruffly. "The bar was closed, no one around gawking, and then they show up. We should have waited them out."

Stephanie tucked her arm through his. "Come over to my place and we'll crack open this bottle."

His brows lowered ominously. "Something has to change."

"That was awkward," Sean said.

"Weird," Blue agreed.

"I don't think I've ever seen her blush before."

"You don't think…?" Jake asked, glancing down the darkened corridor to the elevators.

Sean grinned, "I do think."

"Aw," Jake said, wiping a hand across his mouth. "I don't want to picture *that* in my head."

"Easy for you to say," Sean said. "Both of you with houses of your own. But I get it. Sometimes it's hard to get some quiet time together. It was bad enough before, with me living at Mom's, but now with Philip at Frankie's, it's gotten worse."

"Weren't you and Frankie talking about getting a place and moving in together?" Jake asked as they watched their mother and Max drive away.

"We were, and I guess we still are, but it's more complicated now, with Amber."

"What does Frankie think about all this?" Jake asked as they let themselves out and Sean locked up.

"I don't know."

His brother slapped him on the shoulder. "Well, you'd better find out."

Chapter 10

At noon on Saturday, Louise threw open her front door. Brandy and Amber stood huddled under the porch roof, trying to get out of the rain.

"It's pouring out here," Brandy said, stepping inside and throwing her soggy arms around her sister. "We got soaked just running from the car to the house."

Amber smiled her hello as she shrugged out of her jacket.

"The perfect day for an indoor party," Louise said as she ushered the girls into the kitchen. "Everyone is coming around four, although Maddie and Sarah might get here a little earlier."

Amber still hadn't said anything, so Louise wrapped an arm around her shoulders and led her to the counter where she'd laid out cookbooks, open to the recipes she wanted them to try that day.

"Your assignment, should you choose to accept it," she said in a mock serious tone, "is to recreate these dishes to the best of your ability."

"What are we making," Amber asked, glancing at the books.

Brandy read the titles on each open page. "Mini-pizzas, chocolate cheesecake, and hot artichoke dip. Yum."

"The dip is to snack on as everyone arrives," Louise said. "We should start making the cheesecake right away, though, because it takes the longest. Bake the crust and the first layer, then while it's cooling make the pizza dough. We can finish the cheesecake while the dough is rising, then we'll make the dip so it's warm when everyone arrives."

"I saw a recipe for nachos," Amber said shyly. "I don't remember the exact recipe, but I think I could just make it up. The picture looked great."

"Good idea," Louise said, pulling a stainless-steel mixing bowl out of the cupboard. "I think I've got everything you'd need. Let's give it a try."

Amber took charge of the mixing bowl. "Maybe Brandy could read out the ingredients for the cheesecake and I'll mix it up."

"Perfect," Louise said. "I'll sit and supervise. My back is killing me from cleaning. Oh!" She put a hand on her side and smiled. "The babies are wrestling. I have a feeling these two are going to be a handful. I'm going to need your help."

Brandy put a hand on her sister's belly and grinned as the babies kicked and shoved. Amber watched them out of the corner of her eye, until Louise took her hand and gently pulled her over. "Want to feel?"

Amber nodded and Louise positioned her hand over the most raucous spot. Amber's eyes widened and she giggled.

Louise grinned. "Now, let's get to work."

* * *

At four o'clock, when Sean and Frankie pulled up to Blue and Louise's house, Frankie could see they were the first to arrive. Only Louise and Brandy's cars were parked in the driveway. "Maybe we should wait for someone else to get here."

"No, it's fine." Sean smiled and took her hand. "Try to put school out of your mind for today. The whole point is just to have fun."

He looked relaxed and happy and Frankie tried to echo his mood. At least on the outside. Inside, she couldn't turn off her teacher-brain that said this was her chance to observe Amber in a relaxed environment, to see if her suspicions were correct. She closed her eyes and shook her head. She even sounded like a teacher. No wonder Amber couldn't warm up to her. "You're right, let's go."

Louise was lounging with her feet up on Blue's beautiful burled-wood coffee table, enjoying a cup of mint tea with the girls when Sean and Frankie let themselves in. The house smelled amazing, of chocolate and sugar overlaid with savory Mediterranean aromas.

Louise hauled herself off the couch to greet them, giving them each a hug. Brandy sent them a friendly wave, but Amber lagged behind until Sean grabbed her and pulled her in for a hug, giving her a quick kiss on the temple that made her blush with pleasure. She certainly didn't look afraid of him, and Frankie wondered again what her comment in class had meant.

"Hi, Amber," she said, putting extra warmth into her smile.

"Hi," Amber replied shyly, from the shelter of her father's arm.

"We've been baking," Brandy announced.

"I can smell it," Sean said, smiling at Amber.

Brandy brought a plate of chips layered with cheese and salsa and dabbed with sour cream to the coffee table. "Try Amber's nachos."

"You made this?" Sean said, looking at Amber with pride. "It looks amazing."

She nodded, a shy smile tipping up the corners of her mouth.

"We should be doing more cooking together at home," he said, digging into the nachos. "I've been letting my mom do the heavy lifting in the kitchen for the past few months. Maybe it's time you and I took over."

"Your dad's a wonderful cook," Frankie told Amber. "I can see where you get it."

She was trying too hard, even she could hear it. Amber looked startled by her comment. She obviously connected her with the classroom, not what Frankie wanted today. God, this was difficult!

"So, what games do you have planned?" Sean asked Louise.

"I thought we'd play small-group games as people arrive, then have the pizza, and afterwards have a group game of Pictionary."

"Old school. I love it." Sean rubbed his hands

together. He turned to Amber. "Have you ever played cribbage?"

She shook her head.

"I'll teach you. It's always been one of my favorite games. You play, don't you Frankie? It's a three-person game," he added to Amber.

Frankie saw where he was going. The board was designed for three players and that would give them a chance to have a private round to break the ice. She just hoped Amber's math skills were up to the game.

She needn't have worried. Amber picked up the rules easily and was fifteen-two-ing and four-ing left and right until she was miles ahead of both Frankie and Sean. Basic mental computation was obviously not a problem. Sean was beaming and Amber laughed happily as she whupped his ass.

Blue arrived while they were playing, along with Jake, Maddie and Sarah, who announced, "Grandma and Max are coming later."

The spicy smell of Italian sausage permeated the air as Louise pulled the mini-pizzas out of the oven. "Amber and Brandy made these, too," she said as she put the first batch on the marble topped island. All the kids dove in.

Stephanie and Max arrived while they were eating, bringing Frankie's dad Philip and Max's daughter, Lily as well. Luckily, Steph had given Louise a heads-up about the extra guests, so there was plenty for everyone. Stephanie had told them all about Lily's arrival, but Frankie knew little else about her. She was quiet, but not unfriendly. The dark circles around her eyes bespoke of a hidden problem, probably what had driven her to Fortune Bay, and was obviously still on her mind.

Frankie remembered how intimidated she had been by the large, rowdy Murphy family the first time she was invited to a meal, so she tried to make Lily feel welcome. "Are you going to stay for a while?" she asked.

"A while. I don't know how long," Lily said. "I'd like to find my own place, though. I can't stay with Dad forever."

Everyone stood around the kitchen island, holding plates under the hot pizza slices to stop the gooey cheese from dripping on the floor. Blue followed Louise around the kitchen like a protective Saint Bernard, taking anything she tried to carry out of her hands. At one point, Louise winced and laughed. Blue put a large hand on her belly and above his trim beard, his whole face softened. He was obviously so happy and so much in love. Frankie sighed. He wasn't the babies' biological father, but that didn't matter one wit to him.

When they had eaten their fill, Louise divided the group into two teams for Pictionary, a game like charades where instead of acting out the clue, usually a two-word phrase, the player drew it on a large sheet of paper. Blue carried an easel holding a large layout pad into the middle of the room. They always played a children's version in deference to the kids, but everyone agreed it was difficult enough.

One person would draw a card and the rest of the team would guess. Stephanie was elected to be the timekeeper and Frankie would hand out the cards and replace them in the box when each player's turn was over.

They went back and forth between the two teams, each player taking a turn. Sean went first and was very frustrated when his team of Frankie, Amber, Louise Blue and Brandy were laughing so hard they failed to guess 'mountain climber' in the allotted time. Sarah made sure that didn't happen to her by abandoning the drawing pad after a few seconds and acting out 'lawn mower', ignoring the cries of, "Not fair," from the opposing team.

They worked their way through each team until finally it was Amber's turn. She looked nervous, Frankie thought, as she chose a card out of the box. Amber squinted so hard at the card as she read that Frankie wondered if the girl might need glasses. Wouldn't that be an easy fix?

Amber bit her lip, then smiled. Stepping up to the easel, she quickly sketched a clear rendition of a frog leaping off a lily pad.

"Frog pond," Frankie suggested. Amber shook her head. She drew arrows indicating the direction of the frog.

Sean said, "Frog jumping." Amber excitedly indicated switching the order of the words.

"Jumping frog," Sean shouted triumphantly, throwing his hands in the air.

"Yes!" Amber cried.

She passed the card back to Frankie who glanced at it as she slipped it into the box. The smile slid off her face and her eyes flashed back to Amber, but Amber was basking in the glow of her father's attention. The card said, *jumping dog*, not *Jumping frog*. Amber hadn't read it correctly, even after studying the card for several seconds. That validated the idea Frankie'd had when she'd looked at her transcripts—Amber had a learning disability.

Chapter 11

The game ended in a near draw, although Brandy complained that Stephanie's team wouldn't have won if Sarah hadn't given so many verbal and physical clues to go with her drawings.

Immediately after the game, Louise brought out the cheesecake. Two layers of chocolate ambrosia with a raspberry drizzle on top. Frankie managed to get Louise alone in the kitchen for a few minutes. "I wanted to ask you about Amber. Does she seem to have any trouble reading the recipes?"

Louise squinted into the air as she savored a mouthful of the luscious chocolate.

"She has a fabulous memory, so she often doesn't even need to look at the recipes. Today, and I guess other times too now that I think about it, she has Brandy read them to her as she works. Why?"

"I told you she's having trouble at school. I think she has a reading problem. Do you think she needs glasses?"

Louise shook her head. "I don't think so. She seems to know where everything is. Doesn't knock anything over. Maybe she should get her eyes tested, though."

"It would be great if that were that easy, but unfortunately, I don't think that's the problem," Frankie said. "I'm afraid she has a learning disability. Maybe dyslexia."

Louise tilted her head. "Sean won't be happy."

"Well he's not happy now, either. The longer it goes on the harder it is for Amber to catch up."

"Of course, you're right."

Sean and Amber came up behind Frankie. "Right about what?" She turned around and quickly put on a smile. Now was not the time to bring up the matter. Tonight was supposed to be about fun and bonding. "We were talking about going shopping. It's spring, I need new clothes."

Louise almost choked on her cheesecake. Okay, so Frankie hated shopping, but Amber obviously needed some new clothes. She knew Sean wouldn't object, clothes horse that he was. It pained him to see the way Amber dressed. He'd told Frankie that Amber hadn't let him take her shopping and was still wearing the clothes her grandad had shipped down from Eagle Harbor when he'd cleaned out her room.

Frankie grinned at Amber. "How about it? You and me, and Brandy and Louise."

Amber shook her head and looked at the floor. "I don't think so."

Frankie gave Sean a playful poke in the ribs with her elbow. "I'm sure your Dad will pay."

"Oh, all right," Sean said, pretending to give in.

Amber glanced up at him from under her eyelashes. "Maybe someday."

Better than nothing. "Let's make it soon, before Louise gets too big to fit into the car."

Amber giggled, glancing at her dad.

Blue came into the kitchen and stood beside Louise, putting a brawny arm protectively around her shoulders. He raised his shaggy brows at her and a radiant smile bloomed on her face. She turned to the room at large and said in a loud voice, "Since we have you all together, we have an announcement to make."

Stephanie was sitting on the couch with Maddie, who had her feet up on the coffee table. The other men were talking in a corner and the girls were giggling on the stairs. The chatter slowly ceased, and everyone turned to Louise.

"As you know, Blue and I are about to become a family." She patted her protruding belly and smiled. "So, we've decided to make it official. We're getting married."

A hoot went up around the room and the first real smile of the night settled on Frankie's face as she clapped along with the rest of the family, truly delighted for Louise and Blue. They'd have a lot on their plate when the babies were born, but Blue was obviously all in.

The smile faded as Frankie wondered—what about her and Sean? Was he all in? Was she? She thought she was, and she hoped Sean could see it. Taking on a troubled teen was a big commitment, and while she might not be as maternal as Louise and Maddie—they were off the charts these days—she was trying hard with Amber. She was a sweet girl, under the attitude. She just needed a chance. Hopefully they'd made some headway tonight and for that, she had Louise to thank.

Amber and Brandy left shortly after the announcement, having planned a sleepover at Brandy's house, and everyone else soon followed.

"See you at home, Sweet pea," Philip said as he headed out the door. "I'll just catch a ride with Max."

"Sure Dad," Frankie said. Her father was trying not to intrude on her time with Sean, but great as it was having him in Fortune Bay, the living arrangements had to change—and soon. Before they all went crazy. She was too old to have her dad waiting up for her. In her own place, no less.

"Ready to go?" Sean asked.

"Can we sit for a few minutes? There's something I want to talk to you about, and I think Louise might have some insight."

Sean's face hardened. "You want to talk about Amber. Can't you let it go for one night?"

Frankie could see by the set of his shoulders that Swan was annoyed, but she was determined to see this through. "I'm trying to help her. Come and sit down."

They moved into the living room, along with Louise. Blue made himself scarce, tidying up the kitchen. When they were seated, Frankie started to explain, her excitement growing as she spoke. "I think I've figured out Amber's problem at school."

"She doesn't have a problem," Sean said heatedly.

Stop calling it a problem. "I've spoken to the

other teachers and looked at her transcripts from Eagle Harbor. She does have *issues* with her schoolwork, and ignoring them is only jeopardizing her future."

Sean was seething, but Louise gave her an encouraging nod. Rubbing her sweaty palms on her jeans, Frankie continued. "I think she has a reading disability. Maybe dyslexia. You didn't see the card she pulled during the game. It said *Jumping dog* not *Jumping frog.* She couldn't read the cards."

"That was just a game."

"It was, but she's not doing the work in school, Sean, and not just in my class. If this keeps up, she is going to fail her year, and I don't want that to happen." His lips were compressed into a tight line. "It doesn't have to happen if we do something soon."

There was a moment of silence, then Louise said, "I think Frankie's right. When we're cooking, she always gets Brandy to read the recipe to her. Make no mistake, she's not dumb. After she's heard it once, she can recite it perfectly."

Frankie nodded. "She's smart. People with dyslexia often develop amazing coping strategies, and a good memory is often one of them."

Sean's eyes narrowed as he thought. "But if she can't read…"

"It's not that she can't read, per se, but the letters might seem to jump around on the page. There are many forms of learning disabilities. She'd have to be tested. But once a person has been diagnosed, there are lots of ways to help them. The school will bend over backwards to give her a chance."

Now he looked interested. "Help her how?"

"Like giving her extra time for tests, maybe testing her verbally or, in my case, finding audio course materials. Sometimes it's as easy as changing the font or the color of the page."

"Develop a strategy," Sean said thoughtfully.

Frankie nodded eagerly.

"Poor kid," Louise said. "It must be hard on her self-esteem."

Frankie nodded again. "There can be so many spin-off problems associated with an undiagnosed case, but there are solutions once the diagnosis has been made. I'd suggest you don't say anything to her this weekend, though. Maybe we can meet after class on Monday." *If she comes to class on Monday.* "And set up a strategy."

That seemed to be a concept Sean could relate to. He sat up straighter and looked her in the eye. "Just tell me when and I'll be there."

The party was clearly over, and they left soon after. On the short ride home, Sean seemed distant and he drove directly to Frankie's house and said goodnight. No mention of his coming in or of her going with him to *the Cedars*, to talk. Her stomach was churning as she let herself into the house. By speaking as Amber's teacher, she was afraid she had further distanced herself from Sean.

Her dad was on the sofa watching TV. Muting

the sound, he looked up and smiled when she walked in. "Nice party. That's a great group of friends you have." His smile faded into a worried frown when he saw her face. "Something up?"

She was glad he was there. She sat with him on the couch and told him what had transpired after he left the party.

"Sean was so angry with me for suggesting that Amber might have a problem—but she *does* have a problem. If it's not dyslexia then it's something else, and whatever it is, we should try to figure it out."

For everyone's sake.

Chapter 12

After the party, Max followed Stephanie into her kitchen, took off his coat and hung it behind the kitchen door.

Stephanie patted his arm. "Why don't you make us both a drink?"

Max spun her around and planted a firm kiss on her lips that was more frustration than passion.

"I don't want a drink," he growled softly in her ear. "Couldn't we go upstairs?"

She pulled away and gave him a playful slap on the chest. "I don't think so. Sean could be back at any moment, and so could Amber. She's just next door. She and Brandy run back and forth at all hours during these sleep-overs. If you thought it was awkward that night at the resort, image how it would be to do the walk of shame down those stairs if either one of them came home."

"Well, my place is out of the question now too," Max said gruffly, pulling out a chair.

"How is Lily doing?"

"She seems good. Thoughtful. Hasn't told me exactly what happened to make her decide to leave. I don't want to push her. I never warmed up to her husband, though. Seemed like a bit of a cold fish to me. I guess she finally had enough."

Stephanie cocked her head. "Do you think she's

left him for good?"

Max nodded as he poured their drinks at the kitchen counter. "I do. She's turning thirty-eight next month and says she wants more than an unfulfilling job and coming home to an empty apartment and a husband who works sixty hours a week. I have a feeling it's more than that, though. She needs some time on her own to think. To get her feet back under her. She's already talking about getting her own place."

"Well," Stephanie said thoughtfully, "the cabin is empty. She could live there for now. Could she handle the woodstove?"

Max brightened. "I think so. I'll ask her."

The phone rang and Stephanie answered. Her heart sank when her sister Megan jumped right in without even a *hello*. "Mom isn't answering her phone. Not all day, or tonight, and not yesterday afternoon, either. I went over after work today, but she wasn't there."

"She must be out," Stephanie answered, struggling to keep the *duh* out of her voice. Her sister heard it anyway.

"I'm really worried, Steph. Where would she go without telling us?"

"I don't know. When was the last time you spoke to her?"

"Two days ago. I was trying to pin her down about the home."

Stephanie winced. "I hope that's not what you call it when you talk to her."

"Well, that's what it is," Megan insisted

stubbornly.

"It's a senior's residence. Get with the times. And, when the time does come, Mom can afford to move somewhere nicer than a state-run facility. But really, I think the decision is up to her."

"Easy for you to say," Megan said. "You're not the one running over there on wild goose chases through rush hour traffic."

"Does she call you and ask you to come?"

"No. But like yesterday, I went because she didn't answer her phone."

Stephanie ran a hand over her forehead. She'd made a trip into Seattle earlier in the week and visited her mother. At eighty-five, Dorothy seemed to be completely in control of her faculties, living the way she wanted. She'd given up her driver's license last year but still had an active social life, walking the two short blocks to the senior's center twice a week and catching a ride home after. She insisted the walk was good for her, which it was. She took a cab to the food store and back and had friends who picked her up for functions at her church. She still missed Stephanie's father, who had died ten years before, but other than that seemed to be doing fine.

"I will try to get in to see her more often," Stephanie said. "Twice a month at least. But I do think she's doing quite well for her age."

"But where is she now?"

"I'll call her right now," Stephanie promised. Her mom might answer if she saw it was her calling and not Megan.

"Let me know if you get her," Megan said, and hung up.

Stephanie punched in her mother's number and listened while the phone rang and then went to voice mail. "Mom. Please call me when you get this. Meg and I are worried about you."

When she ended the call, Max was standing in front of her trying to read the expression on her face. "Problem?" he asked, pulling her out of her trance.

"My mother. She hasn't been answering her phone." She glanced at the clock. "Megan's right. Where would she be at ten o'clock at night? Maybe I should go."

Sean walked in the back door. He looked from one of them to the other. "What's up?"

"Your grandmother's missing, I'm going to Seattle to check on her."

Max grabbed his coat. "I'll drive.

* * *

Stephanie and Max returned from Seattle at noon the following day. Working on autopilot, she hung her coat on a hook and collapsed onto a chair at the kitchen table. "Where could she be? I know she took off because Megan threatened to put her in a home, but where could she have gone?"

"Maybe on a little holiday," Max said, rubbing his forehead.

"But—" She shook her head, her eyes

desperately searching the room as if the answer might be hidden somewhere in the mound of work on the table or the cluttered sideboard.

Max took her by the shoulders and forced her to look at him. "Panicking is not going to help." He squeezed her shoulders gently. "Just breathe. Try some of your yoga stuff."

He was right. Stephanie exhaled until her lungs were empty, then inhaled slowly. "Okay. I just don't know what else to do."

Max stepped away, turning to the sink to fill the kettle. "We told the police, phoned the hospitals. Megan will check the house again later today. There isn't really anything else we can do."

"Thanks for going with me last night, but I have to go back. I should have taken her phone book. I could be phoning her friends, her church."

"We contacted the seniors center. They'll call you if they hear anything."

Stephanie clutched her hands tightly together. "I have to do something."

Max sat down heavily, the old wooden chair groaning under his weight. "Come to my house before you go. Lily's eager to see the cabin." His eyes softened. "If I didn't have to stay here and meet the new chef, I'd go back to Seattle with you."

"I know. You have your own fires to put out." She stretched her hand across the table toward him. "Thank you for coming with me last night."

He took her hand in both of his. "Your

problems are my problems."

An hour later, they had picked up Lily and were walking down the tree-lined lane to the cabin.

"Thank you so much," she said to Stephanie. "I really appreciate Dad letting me stay with him, but it's been more than two weeks. I think I may have overstayed my welcome."

"Nonsense," Max said heartily.

Lily smiled at her father. Stephanie could see the visit had worked wonders for their relationship. They were much more comfortable together than when Lily arrived. "I need to think, Dad, to figure out my next step, and I think I need to be alone for a while to do that."

"Well, honey, I hope your next step will be to stay here in Fortune Bay. I can really use your help with the accounts at the resort."

Lily laughed. "You're not kidding. I've seen your books." Her face became serious. "I'd love to stay. At least for a while."

Stephanie stopped in the middle of the rutted driveway and put her hands on her hips. A shiny, black, vintage Lincoln Continental was parked beside the cabin. "Whose car is that?"

"No idea," Max said.

"Squatters! This is an outrage. I haven't been here in weeks. Who knows how long they've been living here?" She took in the smoke belching out of the stone chimney. "They seem to have made themselves right at home."

Max put a hand on her arm. "Now, settle down. It's probably just a friend of one of the kids. Sean might have told someone they could use the place."

"He hasn't mentioned anything to me."

Stephanie stormed up the cabin steps, arms pumping, with Max and Lily right behind her. She threw open the front door and for once, the sticky old door cooperated, flying open with a satisfying bang.

The woodstove was belching heat. The room had to be ninety degrees. An elderly man was napping on the couch. He sat bolt upright, his thin grey hair askew.

"What?" he asked in confusion.

"I should be asking you that. Who are you?" Stephanie asked imperiously, hands back on her hips.

"Just hold your horses," a woman's voice called from the back bedroom. "You've always been quick to jump to conclusions."

Stephanie's jaw dropped. "Mom?"

Her mother bustled into the room, a vision in a purple leopard print track suit, patting her shellacked curls into place. "Don't you be yelling at Howard. He didn't do anything except help an old lady out." She stopped in front of the startled trio. "Hello, dear. Who are your friends?"

"Mom," Stephanie repeated. She seemed stuck on that one word. She gave her head a shake. "What are you doing here?"

"I'm on the run."

"What do you mean 'on the run'? Don't you

know we've all been worried sick? Max and I spent the night in Seattle looking for you, talking to the police, calling the hospitals—"

"Well that was unnecessary. Can't a person take a vacation once in a while?"

Stephanie's eyes narrowed. "A vacation is not the same as being 'on the run'."

"Whatever," her mother said airily. "Now why don't you make us all a nice cup of tea." She held out a dainty hand to Max—who Stephanie swatted to stop his chortling. "Stephanie has forgotten her manners. My name is Dorothy. I'm her mother, and this is my special friend, Howard."

Max held out his hand. "I'm Max Finster, Stephanie's, ah, 'special friend'—"

"Not anymore," she muttered as she turned her back to the group and filled Augusta's tea kettle with water.

"—and this is my daughter Lily."

"Pleased to meet you," Dorothy said, shaking Lily's hand.

"What are you doing here, Mom? Why didn't you tell me you were coming?"

"Because I'm hiding out," Dorothy said, as if talking to a child.

Stephanie put the kettle on the burner with a bang and pulled her cell phone out of her pocket. Dorothy snatched it out of her hand. "Don't you go calling your sister."

"Give that back. Megan's worried."

Dorothy snorted in a most unladylike way. Lily covered her mouth to hide a laugh. "That storm trooper? She's just trying to lock me up. Put me away. Get me committed."

"It's not an institution, Mom. It's a senior's residence."

Dorothy snorted again. "Not the one she's talking about." She shook the phone at Stephanie. "If you rat me out, we'll just have to go on the lam. Won't we Howard?"

Howard grinned and nodded. "Anything you say, Dottie."

Stephanie stopped as she realized they were enjoying this escapade. And why not? Nice to know life could still hold some adventure at eighty-five.

"I'm not going to rat you out, Mom. But Megan's really worried, and she'll drive all the way over to your house tonight looking for you. She wouldn't have to if you'd answer her calls."

"Why should I, just to hear her bully me some more?"

"Now, settle down. Why doesn't everyone just sit down, and we'll have some tea." Stephanie set the tea things on the yellow Arborite table, pairing the cups to their saucers as best she could. Not all of them matched.

Dorothy's voice gentled. "Mom's old cups," she said, then giggled. "I do."

Stephanie looked at her sharply. "Do what?" This was what she'd been afraid of, that Megan was right. That their mother really was losing her mind.

Dorothy waved her question aside. "I wasn't talking to you. Why don't you play 'Mother'?"

Knowing that meant *pour the tea*, Stephanie obliged, still watching her mother out of the corner of her eye. Dorothy smiled softly and nodded. Dust seemed to sparkle in a shaft of sunlight and the smell of sweet spices drifted by, like a soft kiss on the cheek. "Do you hear Augusta?"

Her mother looked her in the eye. "Sisters have a connection, you know. Well, maybe not you and Megan, but Augusta and I always did."

Stephanie nodded. "I remember."

"Augusta was always the sentimental one, kept all of Mother's old china. She was just reminding me how we broke so many of those china cups and saucers when we were children." She chuckled and sat back in the chair, taking in the room. "I like it here. It's peaceful. I think I might stay for a while. Want to stay, Howard?"

Howard nodded. "Anything you say, Dottie."

Stephanie rubbed a hand across the back of her neck and looked at Max. He raised his eyebrows, but his eyes were filled with laughter. And yes, she could see the humor in the situation, too. In fact, it was becoming farcical. Just when they thought they had one awkward relative settled, another moved in. It was never ending. Seemed like Lily was back with Max, at least for the time being.

"But can you manage here, Mom?"

"Why not? There's lots of split wood outside and Howard seems to know how to work the woodstove just fine. We've got everything we need."

They did seem happy, at least for the moment. And it would certainly be easier to keep an eye on her mother if she was here instead of in Seattle. "Well, I don't think it's a permanent solution—"

"Would you rather I move in with you?" her mother asked craftily.

"No!" The image of her already bulging house absorbing two more people made Stephanie shudder. "No. I'm sure we can work something out."

Howard finally spoke up. "Dot and I were tired of living in the city, anyway. This seems like a fine place to settle down. Can we get cable out here?"

Stephanie looked at the defunct black and white TV in the corner and noticed for the first time the small flat-screen sitting on top of the old mahogany cabinet. She shook her head. "I doubt it." She picked up her phone. "Okay, Mom, you can stay here for now, but I have to tell Megan."

Dorothy rolled her eyes. "I know. Megan will be worried that I've fallen and I'm crawling around on the bathroom floor. As if."

Right. As if. So much for carving out a private space and some alone time. Stephanie gave Max and Lily a *sorry* look, but they didn't seem to mind. Lily was chatting happily to Dorothy, and Max gave Stephanie a shrug that said, *what can you do? It's family.*

She smiled at the man she had grown to depend on and stepped out to the porch to call her sister.

Chapter 13

On Monday, the knot in Frankie's stomach tightened as the afternoon wore on and the meeting with Sean and Amber approached. Amber was already acting like a frightened rabbit. If the girl got any more nervous around her, Frankie's chance of a future with Sean was probably finished. But as Amber's teacher, she felt an obligation to help her get on the right road, if she could. That was a given too. She just hoped the two things, being a good teacher for Amber and being with Sean, weren't mutually exclusive.

Building a relationship with his daughter had to be Sean's priority right now, she got that, but to lose him would break Frankie's heart. She didn't have a lot of experience with men. Sean was really her first serious relationship and it had been so hard to bust out of her self-conscious shell and let him in that she didn't know if she could do it again.

And besides, she didn't want to. She loved *him*.

Finally, last period arrived, and students poured in through the classroom door. Frankie felt a nervous flutter in her chest as Amber slunk into the room, avoiding her gaze as she dropped a single sheet of paper onto the desk. Frankie tried to smile but wasn't sure if she'd been quick enough to catch the girl's eye. She didn't want to pounce, but when she saw the page was filled with double spaced lines that looked like it could be the theme assignment for *Catcher in the Rye*, she breathed a sigh of relief. At least that was one thing she didn't have to come down hard on Amber about today.

The hour dragged by. The students were rowdy, always a problem last period, but today they seemed particularly unruly. They were supposed to have finished reading the book and Frankie tried to get them to talk through the themes. She'd managed to skim Amber's paper and was surprised—and of course pleased, although a little suspicious—to see she'd gotten the themes of the book right.

"And what is the point of the ducks," she asked. "Amber?"

Amber's head shot up from where she'd been focused on the book on her desk. Her eyes, still rimmed with black liner, looked like round Little Orphan Annie circles on her face. When it became obvious she didn't know the answer, Frankie quickly moved on to another student.

Her hopes sunk like a stone in the water. Just what she'd feared. Either Amber had copied the paper off the internet, or someone—Brandy or possibly that boy Derek—had written it for her.

When the class ended, Frankie was too distracted to give out any homework. "Amber, please stay," she said as the girl tried to slip by her desk in a pack of students.

Just then Sean poked his head through the door.

A horrified look crossed Amber's face. "Dad."

Frankie wasn't trying to terrify the girl, quite the opposite, so she adopted her brightest teacher's smile. "Please, both of you, let's sit down."

Sean's stomach was churning but he could see the terror on Amber's face, so he tried to mimic Frankie's smile.

"Hi, honey," he said, giving his daughter's stiff shoulders a quick hug before he took a seat beside her at one of the long classroom tables. Frankie turned a chair and sat across from them.

Amber had tears in her eyes and Sean just wanted to take her in his arms, but now that he was seated, it would be awkward if not impossible to hold her. He tried to tell himself this was best for her, but it was like a knife to his heart to see her so upset.

Frankie had a paper in her hand. "Amber, is this your work?"

Amber gulped and nodded.

"Really?" Frankie asked quietly.

Amber looked down and shook her head, *no*. A tear plopped onto the desk. The knife dug deeper, and Sean moved his chair closer and put an arm around his daughter.

Frankie lay the paper aside. "I didn't call your father in to talk about this homework. I called him in because I wanted to talk to you both about the trouble I think you are having with reading."

Amber squirmed away from Sean so she could look him in the face. "I'll try harder. Please don't send me back to Grandpa."

Sean looked like he'd been struck. "Honey, I'd never send you back. Never."

"I know it's important to you that I do well in school."

He took her by the shoulders and looked her in the eye. "It's important to me that you are happy. That's all."

"Well," Frankie said, a little too brightly. "Maybe there's a way you can do both." She turned to Amber. "I think you might have dyslexia. Have you heard of that?"

Amber shook her head slowly, her eyes widening again.

"It's not serious—except in the way it affects your reading. It's a little difference in the brain that mixes up the letters on the page."

"Sometimes they seem to be moving," Amber whispered.

"That must make it difficult to read your assignments," Frankie said gently. Amber nodded.

Sean looked at the woman across the table from him who was trying so hard to help his daughter and his heart swelled in his chest. He had never loved her as much. He might never have figured this out on his own and at some point, Amber could have just given up and ended up on the street, like her mother. His eyes went dry and his breathing shallow at the thought.

He couldn't do this alone. It had been a mistake to keep Frankie at a distance. He needed her, and

Amber needed her. They were a team, but they should be more than that—they should be a family. He vowed to rectify the situation very soon.

"I thought we might try this, for now," Frankie said, handing Amber a flash drive. "There is an audio version of the book on there, along with a recording I made of the questions in both your last assignment and the next one. You can put it in your computer, listen to the book and to the questions, then come in and talk it over with me. How does that sound?"

Amber nodded intensely.

"You can use my laptop and headphones for now," Sean said. "We'll buy you a laptop of your own." He glanced at Frankie for confirmation.

She nodded. "That would be good. There are simple changes you can make to the computer that might help. Like changing the font and the color of the screen. I'd also like you to take some tests."

Amber froze. Tests had obviously been a terrifying experience.

Frankie leaned across the table and put a reassuring hand on her arm. "Not for marks. Just to see what the issue is and how we can help you. Whatever the results of the test, I know your other teachers would be glad to tailor their programs to suit you. I've already spoken to your biology teacher Mr. Swallow and he's in. But let's get those results first. I think I can set it up for later this week."

Sean watched the emotions rolled across

Amber's face; confusion and suspicion, but also hope and relief.

"Thank you," he said to Frankie. It wasn't enough but he didn't know what else to say. She was a miracle worker.

Frankie watched Sean and Amber walk away together down the hall. Sean's relief was evident in the bounce in his step and Amber was talking a mile a minute. Both good signs, but Frankie wasn't sure it had been enough to save their relationship. Sean had been so focused on Amber and how they could help her, he'd hardly even said goodbye.

Chapter 14

The following Monday after class, Amber stopped at Frankie's desk, waiting until the other students had gone before she spoke. They had already had one meeting during which Amber had been positively buoyant. She had listened to the book at home and after a fruitful, in-depth discussion of the themes, seemed right on track with the assignments.

It must be such a relief, like having a blindfold removed and finally understanding what everyone else was talking about. No wonder she'd gotten so tired over the course of a normal school day when every class was a struggle.

Frankie smiled. "How's it going?"

"Good." Amber's smile warmed Frankie's heart. Maybe she couldn't have both the girl and her father, but at least she could be proud of having helped her so profoundly. She *was* a good teacher.

Amber smiled shyly. "I heard you're having an engagement party for Louise and Blue on Saturday. I wondered if you need any help."

"You're invited, of course," Frankie said. "And I guess you've heard about my cooking disasters. I can use all the help I can get."

Amber's cheeks turned scarlet. "I didn't hear anything. I just like to help."

Frankie laughed. "Don't worry, it's not a secret.

I'd love your help."

"And I was wondering," Amber said, looking down and tracing a circle on the desk with her fingertip. "Could we go shopping, like you mentioned that time? I'd like some new clothes for school, and maybe something to wear to the party. Dad said I could ask Derek to come."

"That sounds like fun. Let's get Louise to go too. She's the shopping maven."

"And Brandy?"

Frankie nodded. "And Brandy. We could go after school on Wednesday. The stores are open late. Why don't you tell your dad and Brandy and I'll ask Louise?"

Amber's smile was bright as she bounded from the room.

Frankie pulled out her phone and called Louise. "Feel like going shopping?"

"Clothes shopping? Always."

"Amber asked me to take her and Brandy to get some clothes. Something for the party."

"Sure. I need some new clothes too. I'm busting out of all my pants. Even some of the maternity ones. What's with these women who put on ten pounds and call it a baby?"

Frankie grinned. "Maybe they're not having twins." She thought a moment. "I'm in a fashion rut myself. I could use something new, too."

"You're on."

* * *

Thursday evening, Sean's face appeared at Frankie's sliding glass doors. Nice of him to fit her into his busy schedule. In the week and a half since she'd shared Amber's test results with them, Frankie hadn't heard from him. He'd walked away with barely a word and ever since, a pilot light of hurt and anger had been flickering in her chest, just below her heart.

He slid open the door. "May I come in?"

"Sure," she said, not getting up from the couch to greet him.

Sean looked tired, but the lines of worry around his eyes had eased. He came over and sat beside her on the couch, gave her a kiss on the cheek and, with a weary sigh, sank back into the soft cushions.

"Sorry I've been missing in action, but with the resort about to open and Amber's new regime, I've been up to my neck every day. I really want to thank you. You were right. Finding out that Amber has dyslexia has been a good thing. Now at least we can work on it. And she's so much happier. Relieved, I think. She's opening up to us more every day. It's been great, really cleared the air. And thank you for taking her shopping. I guess that's not a dad-thing."

"Glad to help."

Sean wiped a tired hand across his forehead. "The resort will open in two weeks and then, hopefully, things will slow down at work.

Although, there will still be lots to do. We have to keep the publicity rolling to make sure the first season is a success."

Right. How often will she see him then? She couldn't keep this relationship going alone. How long had it been since they'd been on a date? Their dates were usually just meals at her house, but even that was a thing of the past. And sleeping together? *Ha!* She couldn't remember the last time *that* had happened.

"I hope you're coming to the engagement party for Louise and Blue on Saturday night," she said. "Amber's offered to help."

"Of course I'm coming."

He made it sound like she should know. How could she? She didn't have any idea what his schedule or his life was like anymore. "What are your plans for Easter, Sean."

He looked taken aback. "No plans," he said carefully, as if he'd finally figured out she was pissed off.

And yes, she was pissed off. She'd bent over backwards to bond with Amber—hell, she'd taken her shopping! —and he still wasn't making room for her in their lives. "What about summer holidays? And Christmas?"

"I've been too busy to make any plans." He sat up straighter on the couch, pulling away infinitesimally, but even so, the movement spoke volumes. "What is this about?"

"The future, Sean. I need to make plans for the

future."

"We had plans—"

"Did we, Sean?"

He hitched back to look her in the face. "Of course we did. At least I thought we did."

Frankie crossed her arms defiantly on her chest. "I hardly remember."

He took a deep breath. "I see you're upset—"

"You're darned right I'm upset." *And getting more upset every minute.* "Do I fit into your plans at all? I used to think so, but now I don't know."

He closed his eyes, a patronizing gesture that cranked up the pilot light to a full flame, making her blood boil.

"Do we have to talk about this right now? In a couple of weeks—"

"I'm tired of waiting, Sean."

"I think we should put this on hold and talk about it another time. When you've calmed down."

"If that time ever comes," she muttered, looking away.

"Okay. This is not productive. We'll talk later. Goodnight." He stood up and walked to the door.

Arms still crossed on her chest, she let him see himself out.

* * *

Still reeling from the argument with Frankie, Sean went to Jake's. He knocked on the back door and let himself in. His brother and Blue were watching a basketball game, but other than that, the house was quiet. Thank God. He was glad to get away from demanding, confounding women and sink into the comforting, guy-time atmosphere at Jake's. Just like old times, before they had women confusing and complicating their lives. These guys didn't expect him to talk. Not like Frankie.

"Do you guys have plans for Easter?" he asked.

"Huh? What?" Blue asked.

"Easter? No plans." Jake's eyes never left the TV.

"Right. That's what I said, and she jumped down my throat."

Jake shot him a look. "Frankie?"

Sean nodded and then dropped his head back on the top of the cushion. "I don't know what's gotten into her lately."

Blue and Jake exchanged a look.

"What?" Sean demanded.

"Nothing," Jake said, eyes back on the screen. "It's just that you've always been the expert on women. Until lately."

"That's because this one doesn't make any sense. I thought she understood we were together, just not right now. I've got things to do, work's crazy, and this whole thing with Amber's been way more demanding than I thought it would be."

"Sounds like Frankie might be feeling left out," Blue said.

"Why? What has Louise told you?"

"Louise? Nothing. But hell," he laughed, a deep rumbling laugh. "I'm a sensitive guy."

"Frankie was amazing at figuring out Amber's problems at school. I hate to think what would have happened if we hadn't gotten to the bottom of it." Sean shuddered at the thought of Amber falling into the same life as her mother had on the streets of Seattle.

"Did you thank her?" Jake said.

"Yeah, I thanked her," Sean said, but he didn't sound too sure, even to himself.

"I mean *really* thanked her."

"It's hard to get any time alone with the family around all the time. It's choking us."

"You've got to make an effort. You're the one who taught me the value of flowers, remember?" Jake said.

"Yeah, right. Flowers." Dating 101. How had he forgotten? "I thought we were past that."

"You're *never* past that."

"I thought we had plans. Together. But tonight, she said she didn't think so anymore."

"That sounds serious.," Jake turned and looked at his brother. "You better get your head back in the game."

"We'd need a bigger place. I've been looking, but there's nothing listed. I want lakefront, but prices have gone through the roof in the last few years. Know of anything for sale?" The other two men both shook their heads.

Sean leaned back, relieved to have a plan. It wasn't much, but it was something. "I'll look on the weekend."

"Does she want to move?" Blue asked.

"I don't know."

"You'd better find out."

Chapter 15

When the sliding door clicked shut behind Sean, Frankie's shoulders slumped as the anger rushed out of her leaving a hollow hurt inside. Her dad was playing darts with Max at the Cedars and could be gone for hours. The house seemed too quiet. She could count her heartbeats along with the ticking of the clock on the wall.

Her brain couldn't let the problem go: now that she and Amber had become friends, shouldn't that have cleared the way for them to be together as a family? Or maybe it was already too late. A few tears spilled over at that thought. Maybe Sean wasn't really *all in*, was just coming over when it was convenient, didn't understand what this separation was costing her.

She wrapped herself in a blanket, turned on the TV, and found *Gilmore Girls* reruns on Netflix. She watched one episode, then another, and was just starting on a third when Maddie knocked on the front door and let herself in. She stopped in the kitchen and shook her head as she appraised Frankie's cocoon on the couch.

"Looks like I got here just in time," she said, pulling out her phone.

"Who are you calling," Frankie asked dully.

"Louise." She half-turned away and spoke into the phone. "Hi. Can you come over...She's binging...No, not Ben & Jerry's, *Gilmore Girls*. But if you have some B&J, bring it."

Minutes later, Louise's jeep pulled into the driveway. Soon all three women were lined up on the couch, eyes glued to the screen, each cradling a big bowl of Chunky Monkey.

A tear dripped from Frankie's cheek into her ice cream. "It's happened. The spark is gone." She sniffed, hitching her head toward the TV. "We used to be just like Luke and Lorelai, although Sean has always dressed better than Luke. But he took care of me, just like Luke does."

"You don't need taking care of anymore. You are a strong and independent woman," Louise said, waving her spoon for emphasis.

"But I love him, and he's gone."

"He's not gone. He's just preoccupied."

Frankie shook her head. "I think it's over."

"Is that what you want?"

"No." The word sounded embarrassingly like a whine. "You know I'm not very good at this sort of thing."

"You're good. You managed just fine the last time. He needed a nudge then, too, remember? Time to unleash your Inner Goddess again."

"I don't think Sean would even notice now."

"He's preoccupied, honey, not dead. You've got to jar him out of his work-trance. Sounds like things between you and Amber are good now. Wasn't that the problem before?"

"I thought so. Now we get along fine. That

shopping trip was a breakthrough."

"Finding out she has dyslexia was the breakthrough," Maddie corrected.

Frankie nodded. "We've had a couple of breakthroughs. In fact, I see more of Amber now than I do of Sean. I know he's busy. It would be different if we were living together; if we could talk over dinner, touch base at breakfast, have sex occasionally. But without that, we've drifted so far apart…"

"In a few weeks, when the resort opens, things will change."

"I don't think so. I asked him about his plans, specifically about his plans with *me* and he said he didn't have any. Amber used to be the problem but now I think *I* am the problem." She thought for a minute, licking the cream off her spoon. "Or maybe *he's* the problem. He's thirty-five and has never been in a committed relationship. I used to think it was because of Amber, but maybe it's not. Maybe it's something else. Maybe he just can't commit."

When the other women didn't comment, Frankie sank further into the soft cushions and fixed her eyes back on the TV, where Luke and Lorelai's relationship hit the skids and Lorelai did them one better by eating the ice cream straight out of the tub.

When their bowls were empty and the credits rolling, Louise hoisted herself off the sofa. "Men can be dense. Sometimes you have to hit them over the head to get their attention. It's up to you, honey. It's time to step up. Time to decide what *you* want, and then go out and get it." She pulled Maddie to her feet, and they both kissed Frankie on the cheek as if she was an invalid and left her wrapped in her blanket as they headed home to their families and bed.

After her friends had gone, Frankie sat on the couch, thinking. She wanted what they had, a home and a family, and she wanted it with Sean. That meant Amber too, and she was all in for that. That had been their plan.

She couldn't blame Amber, or Philip or even Sean for what was going on. Sean may not have had any committed relationships in the past, but neither had she. Looking back, she could see she had done her usual thing and at the first sign of a problem, had pulled her head into her shell like a turtle, waiting for someone to coax her out. Sean had pulled her out last fall and coaxed her to reunite with her dad, but he wasn't going to be the one to do it this time. No, this time it was up to her.

Impatiently, she threw off the blanket and got up off the couch. After disposing of the telltale ice cream bowls and wine glass in the dishwasher—because yes, there had been wine too, at least on her part—she went into the bedroom and looked at the dress she had bought yesterday at Louise's insistence. Clingy black jersey with a bit of sparkle around the scooped neck, it was her first 'little black dress'. *And about time.* She'd wear it to the party—it was her house, her party, she could wear what she wanted and go barefoot if she pleased. It might be time to kick it up a notch and break out the diamond earrings from her dad that she saved for special occasions.

When she went back to the living room, her father was waiting.

"I was hoping you hadn't gone to bed," he said, an unusually sheepish smile on his face. "I wanted to tell you—I'm moving out."

"You've found a place?"

"Sort of. I'm going to rent one of the new cottages at the resort from Max for a while. It's time. You kids need your privacy—"

"No, Dad, it's been fine."

"—and I do too."

That got Frankie attention. What did he need privacy for? A girlfriend?

Philip cleared his throat. "Ellen, I mean Cookie, is coming out soon and, well, we'd be too crowded here."

Frankie leaned forward excitedly. "I can't wait to see her! But where will she live?"

"In the cottage, with me. Just for the first little while. They are quite roomy and we've, well, we've been living alone together for a couple of years now. I let the rest of the help go, but Ellen and I, well, we…"

Frankie's eyes widened. Her dad and Cookie? She would never have guessed. But why not? "Dad, that's fantastic. She's always been like a mother to me."

"I know. She's the one who encouraged me to come out and see you last year. She's really missed you. And once she gets here, we'll figure out our next move, together." He laughed, rubbing a hand on the back of his neck. "I have to admit, I didn't know how you'd take the news."

Frankie threw her arms around his neck. "I am so happy for you. When is she coming?"

"She should be here for the party Saturday night."

It was turning into quite a party. She could hardly wait.

Chapter 16

Saturday afternoon, Amber and Brandy arrived at Frankie's a few hours before the party to help. They whipped up Amber's specialty, *Seven-layer-nacho Surprise*, along with cheese straws, and double-chocolate cookies that looked suspiciously like Louise's *Santa's Dark Secret* Christmas cookies and were delicious any time.

Sean arrived alone, with a salmon to barbeque and a giant bouquet of flowers in pink and gold and white—gorgeous roses, fragrant lilies and frothy baby's breath, that eased Frankie's mind about things to come. She suppressed a smile at the look he gave her new, figure hugging dress. She just might forgive him for being an idiot, but she wanted him to stew for a while first.

Amber waved from the kitchen. "Hi, Dad."

Sean smiled. "Hi, sweetheart."

He opened the patio doors and stepped out onto the deck, pulling Frankie by the hand with him.

"I'm busy, Sean. I'm having a party."

"I know. And we're all here to help." She huffed out a breath and glanced at the lake, glad that the morning showers had dissipated, leaving a brisk breeze in their wake and a warm afternoon sun.

"I went looking at houses today."

Her thoughts skidded to a stopped and she

turned around to face him. "Are you moving?"

"Wasn't that our plan? Get a house? You and me and Amber?" He smiled, and the charming old Sean-smile almost worked its magic, almost won her over.

"Were you planning to get any input from me?" He looked flustered. *Good.*

"I was. But isn't that what we'd decided, before Amber came, that we'd move in together?"

"Yes. And of course, Amber is included now, too. But I don't want to move. I like this house. I just wish it was bigger."

"We'll figure something out." He reached for her hands and pulled her closer. She tried to resist but it was hard. It was Sean.

"I wanted to be sure you knew how much I appreciate—how much it means to me—the way you have taken care of Amber. Her whole life has changed. Without this understanding, she could have given up, could have ended up on the street—" He stopped, too choked up to continue.

Frankie softened. "I was happy to do it."

He cleared his throat and put an arm around her waist. "The thing is, I couldn't have done it without you. We're a *team*. I need you. I love you. We need to be together, every morning and every night. *That's* why I'm looking for a house."

"My thoughts exactly," she said softly. Then he kissed her, and with the warm spring breeze whispering around them, it was pretty nearly perfect.

Arms around each other's waists, they turned to look at the lake. The water sparkled in the late afternoon sun and, across the lake, the rocky face of the mountain glowed a copper blush.

"This is a beautiful location," Sean said. "I've been looking, and there's nothing like it available."

Frankie's attention was drawn to a commotion at the front door and she turned to go. "Sounds like Stephanie and Max."

But it wasn't Stephanie and Max. It was her father and—wow! Was that Cookie? Gone was her old, low, no-color ponytail, pulled tightly back from her broad face. Instead, she had a chic, new, blonde bob that went with the flattering skinny jeans and the long flowing top she wore under a lux bomber jacket. Frankie scarcely recognized her old friend.

"Francesca," Cookie said. The voice was still Cookie, and Frankie flew into her open arms. "Or should I call you Frankie now?" Cookie asked, squeezing her tight.

Frankie laughed. "Either. But what do I call you? Ellen will take a bit of getting used to."

"You can call me whatever you like."

Then Stephanie and Max walked in with Lily. Frankie took the platters of food out of Stephanie's hands and left her dad to introduce Cookie.

Frankie found Brandy alone in the kitchen. "Where's Amber?"

Brandy pointed to the back deck where Amber and Derek were talking to Sean. Derek had worn a respectable, blue chambray shirt and seemed to have put most of his swagger aside for today. Although he was a full head taller than Sean, Sean had put his best dad-face on and managed to look seriously intimidating. Frankie grinned. This was just the beginning of his dad-troubles.

The weather cooperated and as the guests poured in, the wind dropped and the sun shone on the lakeside deck, drawing everyone out into the unseasonable warmth.

Sean took control of the barbeque and looked right at home with the backdrop of the glowing mountain across the lake. Dorothy, her rhinestone studded t-shirt blazing in the sunshine, had walked over from the cabin next door with Howard, bringing a shimmering bowl of *Lime Jell-O and Grated Carrot Salad*. Augusta's recipe.

Stephanie whispered to Frankie that she'd taken her mother to see the senior's apartments in Majestic and both Dorothy and Howard had been thrilled with the facility. Especially the indoor pickle ball court. She thought they should be able to get into one of the units in a couple of weeks.

As a guest of honor, Louise quickly ensconced herself in her favorite padded deck chair. She was beaming, as was Blue. They planned to hold the wedding in June, after the resort opened and before the babies were born.

"I want to enjoy my wedding," Louise said. "I don't want to leak milk all over my wedding dress or spend the whole reception changing diapers."

Brandy circulated with trays of appetizers that Amber was whipping up in the kitchen. Derek was helping by plating them, although Frankie suspected he was eating as much as reached the platters. That boy could really eat.

Sean shadowed Frankie silently for most of the evening, but she couldn't deal with him now, not with a house full of people. Quick kisses and secret smiles would have to hold him.

They spread out the food on the marble island, Sean's barbequed salmon, Augusta's jellied salad, Maddie's veggie laden pasta salad and fresh greens from Stephanie's garden. Philip had picked up a roasted chicken and fresh asparagus that someone had steamed while she wasn't looking. They ate wherever anyone could find a seat. It was a feast to remember.

Sean ate standing beside Frankie's kitchen stool. He was unusually silent. Suddenly he put down his plate and walked away, down the hall, past the bathroom and Frankie's bedroom doors. At the end of the hall, he stopped and stared at the blank wall.

Curious, she followed him. He put an arm around her waist and pulled her close. She melted into his side, relieved to find they still fit perfectly together.

"What are you looking at?" she asked.

He dropped a kiss on her temple. "Our future."

She looked at the wall. "What you are talking about?"

He turned to face her and taking both of her

hands in his, beamed as if he'd figured out the secret of life. The stress and worry lines of the past few months fell from his face leaving her old Sean in their place. "I can't do this without you, Frankie. I don't *want* to do this without you. You know I love you. Will you marry me?"

He was crazy. Proposing to her now? In the hall? After all they'd been through—wham! — *will you marry me?*

But hey, who cares where they were? She threw her arms around his neck. "Of course I will."

He held her close and whispered softly in her ear, "Me and Amber?"

She pulled back and looked him in the eye. "It couldn't be any other way. But where will we live?"

"Right here."

"Oh, Sean, I love this house, but there's not enough room."

Behind them, the party had become silent. Frankie looked over her shoulder saw Jake walking toward them, a big grin on his face. He outlined the shape of a rectangle in front of them. "Right about here?"

Sean nodded. "You got it."

Blue was right behind him and Frankie squeezed closer to Sean as the hallway suddenly became cramped.

"We could have it done by summer," he said in his rumbly voice.

They'd lost her. "What done?"

"The family room," Jake said.

"And music room," Blue added.

Sean turned her to face the wall, put one arm around her shoulders and gave her a squeeze. "And upstairs, a master bedroom with a view of the lake."

Suddenly she could see it, a doorway leading to a big, welcoming family room with the sun streaming in. The doorway to her future.

The love in her heart overflowed to encompass all three of these men, as well as everyone in the room behind them. Her family.

"Could there be another bedroom?" she whispered.

"A nursery." Sean nodded, and gave her a kiss, a quick one because Amber had run up and squeezed into the circle. "What are we doing?"

Sean and Frankie drew her into a group hug. "We're getting married," Sean said. Frankie held her breath. For this to work, Amber had to be all in.

She was still for a moment then squealed, high and long, a grin splitting her face as she took off back to the party to tell everyone.

A moment later, they could hear Stephanie call from the dining room, "Another wedding. Wonderful!"

* * * * * * *

Thank you for reading!

If you enjoyed the book, I'd appreciate it if you would leave a review on Amazon, on the page for this book, ***Family Matters***. A good review, no matter how short, is like gold to an author today.

The next Fortune Bay book is ***Starting Over***, Lily and Mason's story. You can read a sneak peek of that story on my website at

www.judithhudsonauthor.com/ fortune-bay-books/starting- over/

Thank you for reading Fortune Bay books!

Judy Hudson

The Fortune Bay Series

Lake of Dreams
Get this free prequel e-novella when you sign up for my readers group at www.JudithHudsonAuthor.com

Summer of Fortune
Book One
Maddie and Jake

The Good Neighbor
Book Two
Frankie and Sean

Home for Christmas
Book Three
Louise and Blue

Family Matters
A Sequel Novella
Everybody!

Starting Over
Book Four
Lily and Mason

Starlight and Tinsel
A Christmas novella
Star and Harry

Also by Judith Hudson

The Secret at Elk Horn Lodge

And writing as

J.M. Hudson

The Rocky and Bernadette Mystery Series

Temple of the Jaguar

A cozy travel mystery.

Murder in the Piazza

Coming in 2022

Family Matters is a work of fiction. Names, characters, places and incidents are entirely the product of the imagination of the author or are used fictitiously. Any resemblance to actual events, locales or persons, living or dead, is entirely coincidental.

Copyright

ISBN: 978-0-9951704-8-3